OWNED BY THE BERSERKERS

THE BERSERKER SAGA
BOOK 11

LEE SAVINO

SILVERWOOD PRESS, LLC

FREE BOOK

Get two secret Berserker books, Bred by the Berserkers and
A Berserker Birth, available exclusively to you:

OWNED BY THE BERSERKERS

My life changed the night the Berserkers took me. Dagg and Svein cared for me like no other--until the Corpse King attacked and the battle rage took their minds.

Now I'm alone. My mates are lost to madness, and my visions are growing worse. My nightmares, my only companions--unless I can defy the pack and save my warriors. I must trek into the wilderness and claim them for my own--or die in the attempt.

Author's Note: Owned by the Berserkers is a standalone, full-length MFM ménage romance starring two huge, dominant warriors who are all about their woman. Read the whole best-selling Berserker saga to see what readers are raving about...

F ern

COLD. *Fingers of ice digging into my bones cold. I ran through the darkness, dodging shadows, my only companion my pounding heart and clutching fear.*

A shape loomed ahead, blocking my path. Clad in rags and white mist, the wraith extended its skeleton hand—

"Fern. Fern, wake up."

I gasped, clutching at air and shooting up, nearly bashing into the person leaning over me. Juliet's worried face hovered close. "Shhh, Fern, you're all right. We're all right. We're safe."

The lodge was dark but warm, the fire embers glowing on the hearth. The shadows along the roughhewn logs were friendly. Slowly, I relaxed. My back ached, my muscles cramping as if I had been running for my life.

"Here," Juliet offered me a cup, and I wet my lips a few times before I let the liquid slide down my knotted throat.

"Bad dream?" Juliet stroked my back. Even though she was only a few years older than me and the rest of the orphans, she cared for us like a mother.

I nodded and didn't say more.

"You seem to have a lot of them," she murmured, but didn't pry, and I was grateful. I'd had nightmares since I could remember. At least this one had come at night and stolen only my sleep.

Juliet's touch and the water helped calm my pounding heart. All around us, the other girls lay sleeping. As one of the older ones, more woman than child, I had my own pallet. It was colder than sharing a bed with my orphan sisters, but at least my night terrors wouldn't wake them.

"Let me know if you ever want to talk about them," Juliet said before giving me a squeeze and slipping back to the big bed she shared with the three smallest girls.

Her kind touch lingered as I lay back down, but I swallowed despair. My dreams were my own, I could never tell her or any other. They were too real. Even now, when I closed my eyes, I had to fight not to go back into the darkness of the dream, where the skeletal hand still reached for me.

"I'm safe," I repeated. "I'm safe."

I lay awake until morning, which came all too soon. The lodge filled with the chatter of the young women and girls. Since being taken from the abbey by the Berserkers, we lived together in a lodge, guarded carefully by the great warriors.

"Fern, You're so quiet today," chirped Violet.

"She's always quiet," Meadow smiled at me. I tried to smile in return but couldn't. My jaw ached from gritting my teeth to keep from shouting of all the horror I had seen. Since rising, the dream had beat at me, threatening to burst from my lips. But I didn't dare speak.

I'd had dreams, visions, since I was very young. My mother died soon after I was born, my father was unknown, but a family had taken me into their care. At least, until I shook with the Sight and told them what I'd seen. Then they'd called me a demon child and left me on the stoop of the orphanage. I learned quickly there not to speak of what I saw. Not to speak at all.

But my dreams were becoming worse. How long could I hide them? How long before they came to me in the day?

I jumped when Juliet touched my arm. "You all right, Fern?" and continued when I nodded, "Could you go to Laurel's lodge and bring back bread? I'd go, but the little ones will want to come, and it's too cold."

I nodded again. The walk would do me good.

"Be sure to warm up well by her fire," Juliet produced a basket and cloak, and walked me to the lodge entrance. "There's no snow today, but it is very cold."

I opened the door and froze at the piercing howl that greeted me.

"What was that?" Juliet gasped, shivering. She shrank back as one of our guards came inside the door.

"It's all right," the Berserker warrior said in his deep, rasping voice. He loomed over us, bigger than any man we'd ever seen, but his face was kind. "It's just a wolf that lives in the canyon."

"That was no wolf," Juliet said sharply. My eyes went wide. I'd never heard anyone speak so boldly to a Berserker.

The warrior just smiled. "You're right. There are two beasts down there who were once men, but no longer. Now they haunt the woods below."

I sucked in a breath as the howling started again. This time a second voice joined the first, the two twining together to make a melancholy tune.

"Have no fear, little one," the warrior murmured to Juliet. "You're safe with us."

Juliet shook her head, a strained look upon her face. I noticed she would not meet the warrior's eyes, even though he gazed on her with a soft look on his face.

"Will you be all right walking to Laurel's?" she asked me, and I nodded.

"She will be safe." The warrior straightened. "I will personally escort her."

At that, Juliet huffed and met the warrior's eyes long enough to glare at him before turning on her heel and hustling back into the lodge.

I blinked up at the warrior, who chuckled.

"Come now." He opened the door and swept out a hand. "The wind is brisk but if we go swiftly, the walk will keep us warm."

I started down the path, bracing for the haunting sound from the slopes below. The Berserkers had built our lodge on a high mountain ledge only accessible by a bridge. I followed my large escort past two more guards and padded down the wooden bridge and into the woods beyond.

At one point, the path forked, and I hesitated.

"This way, little sister," The warrior called back to me and waited for me to catch up. "The other way leads to a ravine, and a treacherous climb down the mountain. The view is beautiful, though," he further explained. He seemed content to talk. Of all the warriors, he was the most friendly. Jarl was his name.

"Juliet seemed upset by the howling. But other than that,

she is well?" Jarl's tone was easy going, but I sensed his interest.

I nodded.

"Good. Please tell her she can ask for anything she wishes. We are here to see to her needs. Her and all the unmated spaewives," he added, and I smiled to encourage him. "We can bring clothes, furs, wood for the fire. I can fetch bread for the lodge, too, though I guess you wish to travel yourself to collect it, if only to see your other friends."

I nodded again.

"Haakon and Ulf's mate makes the best honeycakes and breads," Jarl mused. "Do you know what bread Juliet likes best?"

I shook my head, and he shrugged. "No matter. We will bring back them all, and I will see which one she prefers." And with that, he started whistling, his long legs eating up the path in an easy stride. I scurried to keep up, wondering what it would be like to be so strong and powerful, to speak and have others listen, to walk in the woods and not be afraid.

The path took us straight to a huge lodge connected to a low building. The smell of roast meat hit me, and I picked up my pace, outstripping even Jarl to dart eagerly through the door.

Inside, a large spit turned over a hearth fire. Rows of tables held trays and platters filled with food, and in the middle, ruling over it all, was the queen of the kitchens herself, my friend Laurel.

"Fern," Laurel cried, throwing up her floury arms. She wiped her hands before coming to grasp mine. "Oh, you are so cold. Come warm by the fire. I have tea and fresh cakes." She tugged me inside. I startled when a large shadow moved from the corner. A huge warrior, half of his face mottled with hideous scars, loomed over us. I was too frightened to let out a squeak.

"Ulf," Laurel smiled up at him. "Hazel's mate might be by soon to pick up bread for her and all the lodges near hers... will you ask him to tell her I need more fennel and wintergreen?"

"Of course, little love," he rasped and stooped to give her a quick kiss before heading outside to greet Jarl.

"Don't be afraid," Laurel bumped my foot with hers. "He's very sweet."

I gave my own nod and smiled, hoping I didn't give offense to her or the scarred warrior.

"How is everyone? I should go for a visit, but every day I have requests for more bread." My friend fussed about the hearth, but I knew she loved her work, and was proud to produce enough bread and baked goods to feed everyone on the mountain. "Are the girls doing well in their new home?"

I nodded, accepting the food and cup she brought to me.

"Please, eat," she nudged me before seating herself nearby. She accepted my silence, chattering enough for both of us. "Sage and Willow and I wonder about all of you, kept so far away. We know it's wise to take precautions but," she shrugged. "The pack isn't as wild as it once was. We're making them more civilized."

I thought of the howls coming from the chasm and picked my cake apart.

"Fern, are you all right? You look worried."

A door to our right scraped open, and in wandered another tall, broad-shouldered warrior, handsome and unscarred. Laurel's other mate.

I kept my eyes on my plate as they murmured to each other. The berserker bond allowed two warriors to mate with one woman. What would it be like, to love and live with two men? To be the one they cherished above all?

I had come close to finding out, once. Before all was lost.

I scooped the crumbs of the cake I'd picked apart into a pocket, to scatter later for the birds. When Laurel's mate moved on, I rose and took up the basket I'd brought.

"I suppose you must be going," Laurel sighed. "Please, tell Juliet to visit anytime. Perhaps you could bring more of the unmated spaewives." She hopped up and started filling my basket with fresh loaves. "And you're welcome, anytime. I can always use more hands in the kitchens. Or someone to talk to while I work." She wrinkled her nose. "Not that you talk very much. But I talk enough for both of us."

I returned her smile, and started for the door, where I hesitated.

"Laurel?"

She jerked up from the bowl where she was washing her hands, surprised at the sound of my voice. I understood. I surprised myself, but it was too late now. I cleared my throat. "May I have some extra loaves?"

"Of course." She bustled about, wrapping up a few more. "Do you need another basket?"

I shook my head. She looked curious but didn't pry. I waited until she'd turned to the ovens to secret them under my cloak. I didn't know how I would sneak them off the mountain, but I'd find a way.

Jarl walked ahead of me on the way back. When we came to the fork in the path, I hesitated.

"What is it?" he stopped when he realized I wasn't following.

My mouth went dry. I'd spent so long holding my tongue, I barely remembered how to talk. "Juliet," I blurted the first thing I could think of. "She wanted me to get her some wintergreen. It grows along here."

He frowned but jerked his chin to indicate we should go. I scurried down the path, praying I'd see the low green leaves along the path. All too soon the trees fell away and we were on a rocky ledge, but, lo and behold, there was wintergreen, growing in the cracks of the lichen covered stones.

I dropped to my knees, making a show of gathering the leaves, favoring the ones with red berries.

"Does Juliet use this for tinctures?" Jarl asked, and when I nodded, he crouched and picked some too.

I moved to another clump. "Don't stray too close to the ledge," Jarl warned, but let me go where I would.

When he wasn't looking, I drew out the extra loaves and threw them over the edge, before I quickly returned to the path.

"Are you sure we have enough?" he asked, placing his leaves in my basket.

I just smiled at him. It was sweet, how much he cared for Juliet. My throat closed, remembering what it was like to have two warriors dote on me the same way.

As we returned on the bridge, the howls echoed below our feet. The wolves seemed to have ventured closer to the lodge. Perhaps they would smell the bread, and, even if they preferred meat, they'd know that someone was thinking of them. It was a small gesture, but it might give them hope.

F ern

THAT NIGHT, belly full of bread, I lay in bed and remembered the night the Berserkers came to the abbey to take us.

THEN

I woke in the orphan's quarters to a noise. —a child's cry.

The nuns were not very patient with us; none but Juliet, the youngest of the order, showed the orphans any kindness. Whoever cried out would only find comfort with another orphan.

My mind still sick with my dreams--large shapes running about the abbey, chasing and terrorizing me and my friends--I padded from my bed, past the sleeping girls, and left the dormitory.

Sorrel stood in the hall with one of the young ones, Violet. The older girl put a finger to her lips. I nodded and held out my hand for Violet's.

A crashing noise made us all freeze. Sorrel whipped around even as I shrunk back with Violet. Outside the window, dark figures streamed across the lawn.

"Go," Sorrel whispered harshly. Half-carrying Violet, I ran back down the hall.

More crashing sounds—windows breaking. Inside the dormitory, girls screamed.

"Not that way," Sorrel ordered, and pushed me another way, down a hall the orphans weren't allowed to roam.

"What is happening?" I gasped.

"We're under attack." Sorrel sounded grim, but calm. We raced along, frightened cries following us. I wanted to ask why the abbey would be attacked—there was no treasure here, nothing but a few nuns and a corrupt friar, and a dormitory full of orphaned girls. I saved my breath for carrying Violet, who was skinny, but still heavy. At least she was too sleepy or shocked to cry out.

Sorrel led us to the far side of the abbey. We passed through another hall of windows, and I gasped at the sight of huge warriors, stalking to and from the dormitory. They entered empty handed and left with orphans in their arms or slung over their shoulders. The girl's night shifts glowed in the moonlight.

"They're taking us." I grasped Violet tighter, and she me.

"Not if I can help it," Sorrel muttered. We ran along, my breath aching in my chest from Violet's weight.

"Sorrel," I gasped, just as a crash came ahead. Warriors kicked in the door of the nun's quarters and entered. Shrill screams burst out with the light.

Sorrel and I pressed against the wall, hoping the shadows would cover us. A moment later, the nun Juliet stepped onto the lawn, flanked by warriors.

In my arms, Violet whimpered. A warrior's head snapped our way.

Sorrel tugged me back the way we came. A shout rose from the lawn behind—the warriors had spotted us.

"Sorrel," I gasped as we raced down another corridor forbidden to the orphans. I didn't even know where we were, but it seemed Sorrel did. "Where are we going?"

"A hiding place. This way."

Behind us, glass shattered and bootsteps crossed the flagstones. The warriors were coming.

Sorrel cursed under her breath, words the nuns would whip us for even knowing. I almost laughed at Sorrel's boldness, but my chest was too tight.

What would they do if they caught us?

Following Sorrel, I nearly stumbled down a stair. A few more feet, and Sorrel drew us inside a dark room. The scent of herbs and honey bathed my face. Great barrels were stored here in the cool damp, along with the herbs used in distilling the spirits.

"Hide," Sorrel ordered. "Under the table."

I crouched, pulling Violet against me. Sorrel knelt nearby, working up one of the flagstones.

My lungs still heaved from running while carrying Violet. "We can't escape."

"I'm not going without a fight." To my utter shock, she pulled out a rope, a bow, and arrows. I knew she was a hunter—the best of us at setting traps to catch rabbits in the gardens but did not know she had such a cache of weapons. If she was caught. the nuns would beat her, and the friar lock her in the tower until he found someone to buy her.

Rising, Sorrel strung the bow and plucked it, readying an arrow.

"They may not find us here. We'll hide, then run to the village," she whispered, and I nodded, scooting further under the table. It was a large, heavy piece, made of wood.

Bootsteps sounded in the hall, and I shrank back into the shadows.

"This way," a rough male voice said, startling in its strangeness. Other than the friar and his visitors, there were few men who came to the abbey.

"There's no one down there."

"I scent a few." Boots paused outside of the door. "Smell that?"

"Aye. Sweet." The voices grated my ears.

Move past, move past, I prayed, but when the door swung open, I wasn't surprised. God did not heed the prayers of a sinful orphan.

Two sets of boots entered. I pressed Violet's face to my breast.

"Come out, little rabbit..."

"Easier prey than rabbits." The warrior chuckled as he came forward. A slight movement from the shadows of Sorrel's hiding place, and the whisper of an arrow. The warrior roared.

"She shot me!"

The other warrior chortled. "Serves you right for calling her a rabbit."

The first warrior growled.

"Trouble?" Another pair of boots came in the room. My heart sank.

"Thorsteinn," the first warrior sounded surly. "This is not your prey."

"Not yours either," Thorsteinn was amused. "More like your hunter. She shot you?"

"A trifle." A snap and the arrow fell to the ground, broken and useless under the warrior's boot.

"Stay back," Sorrel's voice wavered only a little. "I have more."

"Bitch," the first warrior growled. A grunt and he staggered back. I scooted further into the shadows, realizing the warrior Thorsteinn had punched him.

"Get out," Thorsteinn said calmly. "This one belongs to me and Vik."

"We were here first!"

"Get out," Thorsteinn repeated, and the hair rose on my arms. He barely sounded human.

Grumbling, the two warriors left. For a long minute, Thorsteinn didn't move. I held my breath in the silence.

A shadow came to the door, entered. Four legs and golden eyes. A wolf. It ducked his head, peering at us under the table. With sniff, it joined the warrior facing the corner where Sorrel hid.

"Stay back," Sorrel repeated, sounding stronger.

"No need to fear, little warrior," Thorsteinn crooned. The wolf stalked forward. "We didn't come to harm you."

"I'll shoot you."

Thorsteinn just chuckled.

The wolf moved between one breath and another. A strange wind blew through the stillroom, sending shivers down my body. Every inch of my skin prickled with instinct. Sorrel gasped.

"Got her," another male voice came, raw and gravely in the dark. "She's a fighter." A man's bare feet and legs came past the table. There was no sign of the wolf.

"Easy," Thorsteinn murmured. "Hush, little warrior, I'll bring your weapons. We'll let you use them again, once we get you to safety."

Sorrel swore.

"Thorsteinn?" Another warrior called into the stillroom.

"Dagg, Svein," Thorsteinn greeted them.

"You found your prize."

"We did." Thorsteinn spoke over Sorrel's muffled curses. *"But there are two more under the table."* With that casual comment that sent my heart plummeting to my feet, Thorsteinn and the other warrior left. Sorrel's angry voice receded down the hall.

The new warriors came to stand in front of the table. I kept a hand over Violet's mouth but couldn't stop my own frightened sigh. In the heavy pause that followed, my heartbeat skittered to a stop.

"We hear you cooing, little dove," one of the new warriors said. He crouched and golden eyes found mine. Shock reverberated through me at the fey glow of his gaze. *"I am Svein. We're not going to hurt you."*

I shook my head.

"We do not wish to scare you, but you are coming with us." He rose, and I jerked in surprise as the table rose above my and Violet's head. Two warriors peered down at us. Svein had light hair and a narrow face. The other's brown beard went down to his broad chest, and he echoed Svein as he reached for us.

"You're coming with us."

F ern

I WOKE WITH A START. The lodge was quiet, filled with the soft sounds of slumber. My friends lay all around. All but Juliet. I frowned. It was not like her to be missing. She even gave up her own bed in order to share one with the little ones

Gathering the cloak, I made my way to the door.

Outside, a full moon shone over the frostbitten ground. We'd had snow that melted in the few days past, but it was still bitterly cold. My breath fogged the air in front of my face.

A low moan made me whirl. I crept along the side of the lodge. There, lying against the wall, lay Juliet, wearing nothing but her shift and a pelt around her shoulders. Her cheeks were flushed in the moonlight.

I knelt and put a hand to her hot brow. Even in the cold, her body burned.

Closing her eyes, Juliet turned her face away.

"Leave me," she croaked.

I left but returned with a cup of water. I knew what plagued her. The same fever had come on me in the past.

Juliet drank some, her eyes darting to mine over the cup. "Fern, please. Do not tell anyone."

I nodded. If any warrior found out she had the spaewife fever, the Alphas would demand she take a mate.

"Thank you," she closed her eyes again. Her brow wrinkled.

As I left, I noted she clutched a posy of crushed winter-green leaves. Perhaps trying to cover the scent of her heat with the minty smell. For her sake, I hope it worked. The Berserkers had the sharp senses of wild beasts.

When I slipped to the front of the lodge, I realized why Juliet had escaped notice. The guards had left their posts close to the lodge. Laughter came from the bridge ahead where they had a fire going. They were playing the game of polished bones, laughing and betting. A few passed a cask back and forth.

I drew my cloak around me and crept along the slope. When throwing the slop pot over the hill, I'd noticed a narrow path among the boulders. The path did not go all the way into the ravine, but it might help me cross under the bridge, to the place where I'd thrown the bread.

I made my way carefully down the side of the mountain, crawling over frostbitten rocks. The moonlight lit my path the whole way. When it came time to cross under the bridge, I waited until a cloud covered the bright light before hurrying along the path. The warrior's voices echoed from high above, but no one noticed my escape, or caught my scent.

By the time I reached the lower ledge, my body was stiff with cold. I searched a while, wondering if I was in the right spot, far below where Jarl and I had searched for wintergreen. Finally, I stood shivering, staring up at the white face of rock where I was sure I'd stood and thrown the loaves over. The clouds passed over the moon until finally the light broke free, and I could see again.

At my back, the briars were broken. At my feet, a trail of crumbs. Someone had taken my offerings of bread.

I pulled a few more loaves out of my pack and placed them on the stone before heading back the way I came.

F ern

I f any of the girls noticed I slept late the next morning, they didn't comment. Juliet also woke late in the day and went about her usual duties with her face weary, full of strain. I whispered to Meadow, who proposed she and I take a group of the youngest girls to Laurel's home. Juliet agreed with relief.

At Laurel's hearth, I gathered more bread, not the sweet biscuits or honeycakes but harder buns good for travel. No one noticed, though I felt a bit guilty. I left some winter-green for Laurel in exchange.

On the walk back, the girls chattering like a flock of sparrows. They threw back their hoods and skipped along, glad to be out of the lodge, even with a warrior escort. It was a fine, if cold day. Berserkers walked ahead and behind us.

Most of the girls ignored them, but I felt their gaze rest on us.

My friends and I had come a long way from the abbey, where we were unwanted orphans, to being precious prizes of the Berserkers. The Alphas did their best to protect us, decreeing death for any warrior who ventured to close to an unmated spaewife. Our guards were carefully chosen. We could visit our mated friends—as long as we took an escort, and returned to the lodge on the isolated reaches of the mountain. We were caged birds, treasured by our captors, coddled and kept safe until the day came when we came into the mating heat.

When that day came, we'd be expected to take a mate. Berserkers were powerful warriors, fearless and strong and able to stand against almost any enemy—except their own battle lust. The magic that gave them supernatural powers destroyed their sanity. Only a spaewife, a woman with her own magical powers, could tame a Berserker.

No wonder the Berserkers hoarded me and my friends like precious jewels. Over the past century, they'd watched their own friends go mad. We were their only hope of avoiding such a fate.

Of course, for some warriors, it was too late.

The howls broke out as we crossed the bridge. My stomach flipped, and my sight blurred.

"No," I whispered. "Not here." I fought the vision as it claimed me, stealing away my reality.

The corpses advanced as one, a silent army. The monsters ran to meet them, filling the world with howls—

Suddenly I was falling, falling. I blinked and came back to myself, amid the girls screaming.

I opened my eyes. My feet were on the edge of the bridge.

"Fern, don't move," Meadow begged. The other girls looked stricken. Violet hid her face.

I swayed in the wind. The howls rose up below me. Then strong arms closed around me.

"I got you," a warrior's voice, rough in my ear. Jarl. Behind us, Berserkers closed around the rest of the spaewives. Each warrior had his weapon out.

"Everyone off the bridge," a warrior ordered. "Into the lodge."

The faster Jarl moved, the louder the howls became. They seemed to follow me. For the last few hundred feet, the warrior broke into a run. My stomach tilted.

Jarl kicked open the lodge door. "Juliet!"

Juliet appeared, face pale. "What happened?"

"She had a fit."

My friend hurried to clear a spot on the big bed, and Jarl laid me down.

"Has this ever happened before?" the warrior turned to the former nun.

I shook my head frantically.

"No," Juliet answered for me.

"Are you sure?"

"Of course, I'm sure." Juliet let tartness enter her voice. "It probably was a bit of dizziness brought on by crossing the bridge. We're not used to such heights."

I lay back in relief as Juliet fussed over me. I kept her secret; she would keep mine. "She'll be all right. You should go help the others. I'll see to her," Juliet said.

"Very well," Jarl said. His rough voice didn't reveal his mood but before he stalked away Juliet turned to him and said in a softer tone, "Jarl... thank you."

A nod and he was gone.

A minute later, and the lodge was full of chattering

spaewives. Juliet held her tongue, closing the curtain to separate us from the rest of the room and turn curious girls away.

I sat with my head in my head, drinking the tea she made me only at her prodding.

At last, my older friend sat down beside me. "You had a vision, didn't you? The dreams have followed you into the day."

I clenched my jaw. It almost hurt not to speak and tell of what I'd seen.

If my visions took over, and I could not hold in my words anymore, would the Berserkers consider me cursed and drive me out? Or just kill me?

"You know you can tell me anything." Juliet lowered her voice. "I won't speak of it to another soul."

I pressed my lips together. I couldn't tell her the truth.

THERE WERE some who believed a witch could speak of the future, and make a vision come true. Witches were destroyed for less.

I spent many nights at the abbey, praying I was not a witch. I felt cursed. If I had any power, I'd make the visions stop. Just to be safe, I'd never speak of them, in case telling them did cause them to become real. If what I saw was Fate, I would not help it along.

After a time, Juliet sighed and left me in privacy. I heard her telling the other girls to leave me alone.

I closed my eyes and willed the dreams not to come.

F ern

*T*HEN

ONE MOMENT, *Violet and I were hidden under the table. The next, the table was gone, and we were in our captors' grasp. The bearded one took Violet, lifting her from my unresisting arms. The light haired one took me. Svein, he was called.*

I stared at his face as he hugged me to his chest and missed the blur of the hallway as my captor carried me away. He leapt from the broken window and landed lightly on the lawn. The one named Dagg strode into the forest with Svein on his heels. The thick canopy swallowed up my view of the abbey's tower. Just like that, the home I'd known for so many years was gone.

The moonlight filtered through the leaves, dappling my captor's face. He moved with absolute confidence through the night, as if he could pierce the very shadows with his glowing eyes. Whenever we ran through a patch of moonlight, his light hair glinted. I couldn't stop staring at him. It wasn't that he was handsome—though he was—but he seemed so fey. As if he'd crossed the boundaries between our world and the next and come with his own purpose—a purpose that somehow included me.

Perhaps I stared because I wondered if it was all a dream.

But no, this was real. Dagg and Svein ventured into the deep woods, and branches brushed my bare legs. Svein tucked me closer. His heart beat close to my ear. He was human, this warrior with a narrow face and sharp blade of a nose, firm lips half caught between a smile and a serious expression as he ran through the glade.

"You're a brave, but quiet one," he said when he caught me looking at him. "Not going to cry out?"

I didn't answer. It was no use. We were kidnapped, taken to who knows where. At least he seemed gentle.

A light flickered in the distance. Both warriors headed there, threading through the thick bracken before emerging into a circle of other warriors. I jerked upright in Svein's arms, coming out of my trance. These warriors had planned and executed a raid on my home. My friends were all captives, or worse. What had happened to them?

My stomach twisted, sick with worry. The other warriors studied me, curiosity written on their rugged faces.

A low rumble in Svein's chest made me glance at him. The light in his eyes pierced me. "Don't look at them," he ordered, and shifted me in his arms, turning me so I'd have to crane my neck to see anyone else. "Keep your eyes on me. I will keep you safe."

I tightened my grip on his leather jerkin and said nothing.

"Svein," a rough voice greeted my captor. "Where is Dagg?"

Svein jerked his head towards the forest. A moment later, the dark-bearded warrior joined us, slinking silently from the briars. Violet lay sleeping against his chest.

He handed her off to another warrior and a tremor ran through me.

"No harm will come to her," Svein promised, his voice velvet in my ear. He crouched near the fire but kept me in his arms.

The bearded warrior joined us, dropping to his haunches close by. With his large beard and thick, dark hair back in a thong, he looked like no other man I'd ever seen. Not to mention his great size and fluid strength. He picked up a stick from the ground and turned it over in his hands thoughtfully, before tossing it onto the fire. All of these warriors larger than an ordinary man. They looked like they could break me in half without trying.

I shivered, and the bearded warrior frowned at me.

"Easy now." His deep voice resonated to my very bones, smooth and caressing. "There's nothing to fear."

I looked down, remembering Svein's mandate not to look at the other warriors.

The light-haired warrior cradled me closer. "It's all right. You can look at Dagg, and me, but no other."

I felt the bearded one's eyes on me.

"I can carry her next," he said to Svein.

"She's not heavy. Barely any weight to her."

I wanted to speak, to ask where my friends were. Out of the corner of my eye, I watched another warrior cradle Violet. He'd wrapped her in a fur pelt of some sort. She slept, oblivious to the warrior's large hand resting on her head, shielding her face from the fire.

At last, I had the courage to sit up. Svein let me, though his firm grip told me he wouldn't let me off his lap. I waited until my heartbeat steadied to look him full in the face. His eyes crinkled, and he cocked his head to the side.

I licked my lips. "My friends. Sorrel..." My mouth couldn't draw enough moisture to speak.

"They're safe." Svein's voice rumbled through me. "My fellow warriors would fall on their swords before treating them ill."

My brows knotted together as I tried to understand. Why had these warriors come? What use did they have for a bunch of orphans?

Svein cupped my chin.

"So brave..." he murmured. "You're afraid but you speak anyway." His thumb stroked my cheek and I flinched away. His touch disturbed me—not because it hurt, but because it felt good. Sensation stirred deep within my body.

Slowly, reverently, Svein stroked my hair back from my face. In the firelight my hair glowed like coals, dark as pitch with sparks of red fire. My hair often drew attention. Another reason I'd learned to hide.

"Beautiful," Svein said and I blinked. "Has no one ever told you that?"

I jerked my head, once.

"You are beautiful," he repeated, and warmth rushed through me like a tide. I stared at him, not knowing what I felt.

"She is the one," Dagg half spoke, half growled. He sounded like a wild animal, but for some reason I wasn't afraid. I met his dark gaze boldly and watched his irises light.

"Yes," Svein agreed softly. "She is ours."

Warriors stood around the fire, muttering, but the three of us were lost in our own world.

I opened my mouth to speak again when a harsh wind blew over us, whipping through my hair. Both Dagg and Svein lifted their heads, muscles hardening with readiness.

The air carried a stench that made me gag.

The next moment, one of the warriors dashed out the fire.

"The Corpse King comes. Run!"

6

F ern

I WOKE to the howling outside. My legs cramped as if ready to run. I forced myself to relax, muscle by muscle, as I listened to the howls. They were almost familiar, twining in harmony both beautiful and sad.

A curtain still separated me from the others. On the other side, a girl cried softly. "Why do they howl so? Are they hurt?"

"A warrior told me they lost their mate," Juliet answered.

"A mate would save them, right?" another girl asked.

"Yes, but they can't claim one now. They're minds are gone. They would hurt her." Juliet said.

"It's so sad," Meadow spoke up.

"What is?" Juliet asked.

"I heard some of the warriors saying that the Alphas

don't want the mad wolves so close. If the mad ones don't leave in a few days, they'll be driven away."

I couldn't stop my sound of distress. Meadow glanced at me and I raised a cup to my lips to hide my expression.

"That does seem cruel," Juliet agreed.

"It does, but the pack has no choice," Meadow continued. "The Berserkers protect us."

Juliet sniffed.

"Would you do it, Juliet?" Meadow asked.

"Do what?"

"Mate with a Berserker?"

"I don't know. I am... was a nun. I made a vow of celibacy."

"But what if it would save them?"

The door opened, and Jarl walked in. His gaze fastened on Juliet, who flushed.

Juliet cleared her throat and rose. "I best see what meat our guards have brought us tonight." She hurried to Jarl, who raised a curious brow but followed her back outside.

"You should not ask such questions, Meadow," one of the older girls muttered.

"But I truly want to know," Meadow protested.

"Then what about you? Would you mate with a Berserker, if it would save their life?"

Meadow flushed brighter than Juliet had. "It depends."

"On what?" the girl asked sharply.

"On whether the warriors wanted me or not. Two men who cherish you above all. Can you imagine it?"

The blonde girl, Rosalind, gave a sharp shake of her head, not quite a negation. Her eyes suddenly sought mine. "Why don't you ask Fern?"

"What?" Meadow turned to me. "Why would you know?"

Fumbling my cup, I gave a weak shrug, and escaped to the back of the lodge.

7

F ern

THEN

I LOST track of how long the warriors carried me through the dark. Dagg and Svein soon separated from the rest of the band, forging ahead as the stinking wind swirled around us. Dagg disappeared for a time and Svein hunkered down to wait. Cold crept in, icy fingers penetrating my thin garments. When Dagg returned, he handed Svein a thick pelt. The narrow-faced warrior wrapped me in the fur before they continued on. Warm again, I pressed my face to the hollow of his throat and slept.

I opened my eyes in the low light. Shifting a little, I peered out from the pelt into a close, dark space. A cave of some sort. Dagg crouched at the entrance, feeding a small fire. His big body shielded the fragile flame from the wind.

"Sleep well?" Svein offered me a waterskin, and a bit of dried meat once I wet my throat.

Dagg came and offered me another pelt, this one larger. He wrapped it about my shoulders and lifted my hair free. "So lovely," he admired. "Little red."

I blinked at him and he lightly tugged an auburn lock. "No more words for us? No matter. We can wait for you to find your voice."

We sat in the cave and rested. Outside the mist swirled so thick, I didn't know if it was night or day.

"The Corpse King is a mage," Svein explained to me. "He casts spells to control the weather, to drive us in confusion toward his lair. We'll hide here and wait it out."

"He wants you," Dagg said, and I believed him, even though it seemed too wild to be true. "He can't have you. You belong to us, now."

For some reason, his claim didn't make me afraid.

As time went on, it grew darker. I stared into the mist until I saw shapes moving into the gloom. I tried to jerk out of my trance, but the shadows sharpened, became a giant skeleton extending a bony hand toward me...

Bolting upright, I screamed.

A dark shape loomed in front of me, breaking the vision. Dagg.

Large hands came to either side of my face. Svein's worried expression came into focus.

"Lass? What was it, what did you see?"

I clung to him. The vision was gone. He'd pulled me back somehow.

"It's all right. You're safe now. We won't let the Corpse King have you."

8

F ern

THE CORPSE KING. I came awake, trying to piece together my dreams and memories. The skeleton hand reaching from the mist—it seemed so real.

It was night. The rest of the lodge lay in slumber. I listened for the lonely howls of the banished warriors. The wind whistled in the eaves, but that was all.

I dozed, drifting.

I walked through a castle, a great hall and a long line of women watching me silently. A king waited on a dais far ahead, but every step I took weighed me down. I wore a gown, and a necklace—a simple chain and a milky white stone. My steps grew heavy, the jewel a weight around my neck. By the time I reached the stairs to the dais, I felt like I was pushing through water. The women watched, but none moved to help me. Finally, I looked up and saw the king—and he was made of bones.

I stumbled back, and the jewel on my breast flared hot. I grabbed it in my hand.

"Yes," the ghost women murmured. But the king approached quickly, murder on his monstrous face. The women around me faded.

"Don't speak," the king's terrible voice echoed in my head. The jewel in my hand pulsed hot enough to burn.

Then the king was looming in front of me. I opened my mouth to cry out and no noise came.

"Fern?"

I startled awake, gasping for breath.

"Easy," Juliet said. "you were crying out."

It was still dark in the lodge and everyone else was sleeping. Juliet had drawn back the curtain separating me from the rest. In the firelight, she looked tired.

"What was it? A dream?"

A terrible weight pressed on my chest. *Don't speak. Don't speak.* I gritted my teeth until tears pricked my eyes.

"Oh, Fern," Juliet hugged me. "You are suffering so. It pains me to see it." Her scent enveloped me, the light fragrance of rosewater. Back in the abbey, she'd tended a whole garden of roses and distilled their essence. Even here, the scent clung to her.

I sighed, deeply, and pulled away, touching her face in thanks. She was kind, but I could not burden her.

There was only one time I was free from the visions. I would give anything to return to that time again.

9

F ern

AFTER THE CASTLE DREAM, I could not stop the visions anymore. They came unbidden, haunting my days. I dared not look into the water in my cup, or the caldron of broth, or stare at the fire. The younger girls grew used to me falling into a trance and made a joke of it. Juliet watched me more closely, worry written on her face. Of all my friends, she was the only one who guessed what was happening. She helped me hide it from our Berserker guard. It was easy, because the weather had turned bad and we no longer left the lodge.

"How long have you had visions?" Juliet asked me quietly one afternoon. We sat in the corner. I'd been tending the fire when the trance come over me. It lasted but a moment, but I'd slipped and burned my hand.

I watched Juliet's fine, white fingers dab salve on my burn, and did not answer her.

"They are nothing to be ashamed of. I know the nuns threatened you when you would speak."

They'd done more than threaten. Back at the abbey, the nuns had locked me up when they caught me in a trance, even beaten me. I learned to hide, to stay silent. But what would happen when my words burst from my mouth?

"Fern," Juliet finished bandaging my hand but gripped my good one. "I think we're truly safe here. The Alphas consult with witches. Their mates train with one... Perhaps you could talk to them—"

I shook my head. My visions were of the devil. I'd be labeled demon spawn and cast out—or worse. The warriors might not tolerate a sick woman in their midst, around their precious mates.

"I am worried about you, Fern." Juliet stroked my hair for a moment and added thoughtfully. "Your hair is so beautiful. You should wear it uncovered more."

I had red hair like my mother's. "A whore's color," I rasped.

"Did the nuns tell you that?"

I nodded.

"That was unkind." She frowned.

"You were a nun," I reminded her gently, surprised she didn't share the same morality as my tormentors.

"I was an orphan first, and even after I took vows, I was the youngest of them and never a very good nun."

I disagreed silently. Juliet had always been pious, and kind, even when she wore the habit. She was a better nun than the rest of them.

"It doesn't matter now does it. I'm no longer one. Even I could not escape my fate."

Did she mean the fate of a spaewife—the kidnapping or the fever?

"God has abandoned me. Or perhaps he never cared."

I touched her hand.

"Oh Fern, what am I to do?" She turned her face to the wall, hiding carefully from the others. It was my turn to comfort her, but I had no advice. The more she went into the mating heat, the more likely it was a warrior would discover her secret. Even though she'd been a nun, Juliet was young and lovely. She was a spaewife, and those were in short supply. When the heat came fully upon her not even a thousand bundles of wintergreen could cover her scent. The Berserkers would find out, and they wouldn't ever let her go.

The door to the lodge opened, and men's voices echoed on the other side of the hearth. Juliet ducked her head and wiped her eyes just before Jarl appeared. His gaze swept over the room, moving until it found and fastened onto Juliet. The former nun raised her chin and met his gaze with a glare.

"What do you want?" Her voice was cool, with none of the tremor it had just moments ago.

"We have supplies. Provisions. Snow's coming. A blizzard."

"Will we be stuck here?" Meadow piped up.

"Perhaps, perhaps not," Jarl answered her, but it didn't take long for his gaze to drift back to Juliet. "We'll be prepared. We're stacking extra wood outside."

"What about bread?" Juliet asked. "Should we visit Laurel while we still can?"

"I'll get it. The flurries are already coming down. Could pick up quickly, and then it's hard to see. Easy to get lost and fall right off the mountain."

"Will you get lost?" Violet asked.

Jarl smiled and squatted so he could look the young one

in the face. "No, I'll be fine. Berserkers have more senses than just our eyes."

"What about the missing warriors?"

"The missing?" Jarl questioned, and his eyes met Juliet's over Violet's head.

"The wolves who aren't on the mountain," the nun reminded him. "The ones who howl."

"Ah. Them. We told the Alphas of the howling. We have orders to drive them away, as soon as the snow stops."

As if they knew we spoke of them, the howling began again. I relaxed, realizing I'd been waiting for the sound to reassure me.

Jarl left soon after, and I crept to the door to peer out. Sure enough, the sky was grey, and white flakes already drifted through the air.

A memory hovered, surfaced. Dagg and Svein carrying me through the mist. I'd braced myself against visions of the haunting skeleton specter, but they hadn't returned. Dagg and Svein kept the visions away. It was the last time I felt safe.

"Those poor warriors," Juliet murmured. She gave me a pelt to tuck around my shoulders and left me to watch the falling snow.

F ern

TRUE TO HIS WORD, Jarl returned with baskets of bread and meat pies. He and a few fellow warriors went in and out with armfuls of wood for the great hearth, stomping snow from their boots each time they entered. When the blaze was built up, Meadow and a few girls invited the warriors to stay and warm themselves. Juliet gave them a sharp look but did not object.

"For a little while, then we must return to our post."

"The Alphas won't expect you to stand guard in a blizzard?" Meadow asked as she and Violet served the warriors hot tea.

"We're used to snow," Jarl told her. "We came from the Northlands, a land of ice and mountains."

"How did you come here?"

"On dragon headed ships that fly over the water." Jarl

winked at Violet and accepted a roll from one of Laurel's baskets.

"Really?" the young one asked.

"It's true. Do you know how the Berserkers came to be?" When she shook her head, he settled in to tell the tale, speaking loud enough for the entire lodge of warriors and young women to hear.

"Long ago, a great king wished to rule the land. He assembled an army of warriors. The best he sent on a special quest."

"How did he determine the best?" This came from Rosalind.

"The king set challenges for all the warriors. We fought in mock battles and competed for his favor. The best of us were sent to a witch who cast a spell over us, giving us great power and even greater fighting skill."

"The witch Yseult?" Meadow asked.

"A different witch. This was over a hundred years ago."

"So long ago? But how are you still alive?" Rosalind scowled as if their long life was a personal affront to her.

Jarl mock bowed. "Magic, my lady. The spell the witch wrought gave us superior strength and speed. We fought for the king and won him a kingdom. But our power came with a price. The magic awoke a beast within, and it grows restless in peace times. If we are not careful, it will drive us mad."

"Many Berserkers have already succumbed," one of Jarl's friends, Fenrir, added. A tall man with a thin scar on his cheek, Fenrir spoke little, but seemed to see everything. Like, Jarl, his gaze often fell on Juliet. The nun ignored both of them, focused on braiding her long, dark, curly hair.

"The magic that made us allows us to form bonds between each other. Pack bonds, as well as a brother bond with another warrior to support each other when the battle rage comes. That is how some of us survived. But it is best for us all to soon claim a mate." Now Jarl looked boldly at Juliet.

"Two men with one woman?" Juliet raised her chin in challenge. "Tell me how that is right in the eyes of God."

"We don't believe in one god," Jarl answered.

"That is blasphemy."

"Not to us." he cocked his head. "Are you upset that we don't worship yours? Tell us his name, and we will add him to our faith. We have many gods. There is room for one more."

Juliet pressed her lips together and looked away.

"I think it is all right for two to claim one mate," Meadow said thoughtfully, "as long as the woman is content. Our friends seem happy."

Juliet rose and left the room. Jarl signaled and Fenrir followed her.

"Is it true the Alphas will force us to take a mate?" Meadow asked.

Jarl paused before he answered. "The Alphas don't wish to force anyone—"

"But they will, won't they?" Rosalind spoke bitterly. "Once we come into heat we will be forced to take a mate."

Jarl spoke carefully. "It's more a matter of what you will desire. The Alphas will protect you from the pack, but the spaewife fever is difficult to withstand."

"And if we get the fever, but still don't wish to take a mate?" Rosalind probed.

"The Alphas do not want you to suffer," Jarl murmured.

Rosalind leaned forward. Her young sister, Aspen, a girl about Violet's age, sat close by. "So they will match us with warriors?"

"They will... encourage you to choose mates, yes. For the good of the pack, as well as for your own relief."

Rosalind snorted. She sat stiff and straight, her long golden hair flowing over her shoulders like a cape. Many Berserkers noticed her, but she ignored them all.

"Is it so bad?" Another warrior with red hair spoke up from his place by the door. "Your friends found mates and are happy."

"At least in the abbey we had a choice. We did not have to take husbands, we could become nuns," Rosalind snapped.

"Yes, but now the abbey is no more. The Corpse King sent forces to take you and destroy it."

"So you say," Rosalind sniped.

"You know it is true," the warrior raised his voice. "You were among the band of warriors that was routed. You and your sister were almost kidnapped. We penetrated the mage's lair to free you—"

"Enough," Jarl ordered. "Tyr, we need more wood for the fire."

Shaking his head at Rosalind, the redhead warrior stalked off. Rosalind huffed and grabbed her sister's hand, leading her to the back of the lodge, away from the warriors.

An awkward silence followed.

"The Berserkers want to protect us, right?" Meadow asked.

"Right," Jarl said with a bit of relief. "The Corpse King would claim you all if he could."

"Why?" Violet asked.

Jarl shrugged. "The witches say he uses spaewives to feed his evil magic."

"But you are strong enough to beat him?"

Firelight glinted off Jarl's eyes as they turned gold. "We

are. We will do everything in our power to keep you safe." With that, he moved away from the hearth, heading out the way Juliet and Fenrir had gone.

"Why do they call him the Corpse King?" Meadow asked one of the remaining warriors quietly, and he answered just as quietly. I strained to hear.

"Because he raised an army of corpses to fight for him. More than that, some say he is a corpse himself."

A hand reaching from the mist. Bony fingers extending from a skeleton...

I jolted out of my trance and blinked.

"Fern?" Violet asked, and I turned away from the fire and my vision. I knew the figure who'd been haunting my dreams. Suddenly, I could not stand to be around anyone. Grabbing a bucket that we used to fetch water, I headed outside. Juliet stood with her back to the wall, looking up at both Jarl and Fenrir. Her cheeks were flushed, and her eyes shot sparks as she argued with the two of them. Their voices didn't carry, and they didn't notice me hurrying past. Grasping a pelt tight about my shoulders, I stepped into the bitter cold. The wind numbed my face, but I welcomed it, knowing it was real and not a vision.

Jarl was right. The warriors who took me from the abbey told me they would keep me safe from the Corpse King. They did, too, until the madness took them, and the rest of the pack drove them away.

By the time I'd finished filling the bucket with snow, the missing wolves were howling again. I could hear the loneliness in their voice.

If I could find Dagg and Svein, they could help me. They could keep the dreams and visions at bay.

I would leave and go to the banished ones. They were my last hope.

11

F ern

I woke just after dark. After breaking bread with us, the warriors had gathered outside the lodge. They built a fire large enough to withstand the snow and stood under the eaves sharing a jug of mead. The rest of the lodge was quiet. Juliet wasn't abed, but that was just as well. Of all the girls, she would guess why I'd gone. Better she not see me leave, so she knew nothing if the Berserkers questioned her.

Carrying only a sack of food and a few possessions, I snuck out the back. My boots were new and tied up my calves, oiled leather that would keep out the wet, but I still felt the cold when I stepped into the knee-high bank of snow. I hurried along the back path, making my way to the place where I left the bread for the banished warriors. For days now, I'd been tossing loaves over the mountain side, slipping out of the lodge under the pretense of looking for herbs. I was as silent and stealthy as I'd been in the abbey, and no one noticed me coming or going. I might as well have been a winter sparrow hopping over the drifts, a brown shawl covering my bright hair.

The snow had stopped coming down. A few flakes danced in the air, blown off the snow-laden tree branches. The moon peeped out from behind a few clouds, but I knew the trail enough not to need to see it. I trekked down the mountain until I came to the lower ledge. There I searched for any sign that any warrior had come here but found nothing. Hours ago, the howling had stopped. I waited for a time, shivering in the deep snow drifts, hoping the wolves would start their lonely call again, and lead me in the right direction. Never had anyone been so eager to seek out two mad beasts. I almost smiled at myself.

Finally, I gave up waiting. Facing the briars, I chose a direction, and started to find my way off the mountain.

Halfway down, it started snowing. Clouds covered the moon and the flurries came fast and thick. I kept going through the blizzard but soon enough I was struggling through the drifts. But I dare not stop. After this storm, the banished ones would be driven away. I could not sleep until I had found them.

After a time—could've been a few wearisome minutes or hours—the snow stopped. High above, I could see the light from the warrior guard's fire. If they realized I was gone, they'd come for me, and I'd never have another chance to escape.

I pushed on. At last the boulders gave way and trees took their place. I plowed between them, and the falling flakes quickly covered my tracks. My feet were numb, as were my hands. My cheeks ached with cold.

Perhaps I had made a mistake. But I had to press on. All

my life I'd been unwanted, unloved. Dagg and Svein had wanted me. I had to remember this.

I stumbled and caught myself. Trudging to a tree, I rested against the trunk until my vision cleared and the world righted itself. That's when I realized the land had leveled.

I'd done it. I'd left the mountain.

Behind me was a slight depression—my trail in the snow. A few more hours and the storm would obliterate it. The Berserkers would have trouble tracking me. Now I just had to survive long enough to find my former mates.

When my legs grew too weary to press on, I crawled under a hemlock. There was no snow under the thick bower of branches. I pushed aside the twigs to lay down in the dark cocoon, a pocket of dry warmth under the weight of the snow. I wrapped my cloak around me and slept.

12

S vein

THICK SNOW PILED between the rows and rows of dark trees. My world was black and white, simple and clean. The cold muted all the smells of the world, except for the sharp sky scent of the falling flakes. I climbed a large rock and rested a while, letting the snow pile higher and higher. I'd woken early to mark my territory, going from tree to tree to splash my scent on the bark, leaving a clean border I'd defend unto death. My territory was all I had left.

The black wolf trudged through the drifts, nose lowered as if he was on the hunt. I waited until he passed the pine grove and approached my standing stone before I raised my head and growled.

The black wolf stopped and gazed at me. His golden eyes were clear, but I knew better. There, on the edge of his scent—the bitter smell of madness.

It wouldn't be long now. We'd spent many nights at the foot of the mountain, banished from safety but unable to leave it behind. How many moons had we greeted with voices entwined in a melancholy song? How many moons since he'd turned on me, snarling, and driven me off as an enemy? Now I carefully marked my territory and waited for the end.

The black wolf cocked his head as if trying to recognize me. I knew him once, but not anymore. Now he was just another monster inhabiting these woods.

I steeled myself for the fight, but in another moment, he huffed and trotted away. I continued on my route, waiting for a bird or a squirrel to venture into the snow and become an easy dinner. The cold didn't penetrate my fur, but my bones remembered it from winters as a child. Blizzards here weren't as mean, but a man wouldn't last long.

Good thing I was no longer a man.

A part of me wished to follow the black wolf and attack. I resisted the urge. Wolves don't fight for the sake of fighting. In this way, they are not like men.

The day would come when the battle lust would rule, but today was not that day.

I leaped off the rock and sniffed my fellow wolf's tracks. We would meet again, I was sure. Until then, I'd keep to my own territory.

I made it as far as the mountain before stopping again. The snow was broken with fresh tracks. By the look of it, the trespasser was small, barely able to trudge through the gathering drifts. Whoever it was, they would not get far in this storm. Easy prey for a strong hunter.

As I came closer, my nose filled with the smell of this prey. Human. Feminine. And something more.

An intriguing scent. I bent my head and followed it.

13

F^{ern}

THE COLD SEARED my lungs as I crept out of my hiding place. It took me a few minutes to push aside the snow laden branches, but at last I stumbled out into a world of white. Working my stiff fingers, I ate some snow.

A desolate landscape, white and barren, stretched before me and behind. I wished the wolves would howl again. Perhaps they were buried. Perhaps they'd died in despair.

With that bleak thought, I pressed on.

$\sim$

SVEIN

. . .

OVER THE COURSE of the hunt, I came to know my prey's scent, fresh and strange, clearly distinct from the blue frost smell of the cold. Each footprint bore a faint whiff of winter-green, along with the smoky tang of woodfire. Underneath, some enticing sweetness, almost floral. Like long forgotten springtime.

By the time I caught up to my prey, I had fallen in the love with the scent. I was drunk with it.

A shape moved ahead, dark and clumsy against the drifts. I slowed and slunk behind a few bushes, but there was no danger of getting caught. My prey was tired, flagging, step by faltering step.

The hood fell from her head, and her hair blazed in the sunlight. Red, bright as a robin's breast.

She fell. Before I knew it, I'd broken cover and rushed to her side. As I drew close, I slowed, stalking my prey carefully.

The young woman's eyes were closed, but it was no mistaking her. She was the one Dagg and I took from the abbey, the one we'd claimed before—

I bowed my head close to her. She was still alive. For a moment, she twitched a little as if she sensed me close. The snowflakes hit her cheeks. The first few melted, but then they began to gather.

The Alphas told us they'd keep the spaewives safe. They'd promised. Why was she here? What drove her out in a blizzard?

Her lips were turning blue. If she stayed out in the elements, it wouldn't be long.

I threw back my head and howled. Slowly, for the first time in months, I drew on my Berserker strength, and Changed.

14

F ern

PAIN RUSHED through my limbs and I cried out. Someone was cursing in a guttural voice, more growl than voice.

"Damn this snow—"

Cold air swept over my body, and I curled into a ball.

"No, no," the gruff voice ordered. Large hands caught my hands and chafed them. Slowly, my fingers uncurled. I moaned at the tingling pain.

"You still have feeling in your limbs. A good sign. No, don't fight me. You're safe now."

I tried to speak, but my teeth started chattering. A second later, he tucked me somewhere warm. Bit by bit, the shivers left me. Again, I tried to mouth a name, but no sound came out.

"Hush. Rest now, little dove." I rested my head against a strong, smooth wall, and listened to the heart beat.

"What were you thinking, coming out in the storm?" The rough voice sounded more human with each passing second.

I snuggled closer to him and let sleep steal me away.

When I woke again, I faced a crackling fire. Night had fallen again. The cold pressed in, the thin warmth from the fire barely holding it at bay.

A shadow stirred at my back. "Lass? You awake?"

I nodded

A large hand roamed over me, finding my hand and squeezing it. "You're too cold. I need to leave soon and get meat."

I fumbled with my clothes until I found the mouth of my sack. My fingers ached, but they worked. The warrior sucked in a breath as I drew out the hard tack.

"Bread? You've been leaving it for us."

I nodded.

Stubble brushed my face. "Oh, lass. What did we do to deserve you?"

He took the supplies reverently. Too tired to eat, I lay back down, and my eyes fluttered closed.

For long minutes I fought sleep, wanting to stay with my rescuer. Warmth crept into my limbs.

It could've been minutes, or hours, but at last I climbed out of slumber and came back to myself enough to take stock of where I was. I lay on my side the warrior at my back, between the warrior and smooth rock. When I turned my head, his fingers tightened on my hip, but he seemed content for us to lie close together. His warmth seeped into me, giving me strength.

"You gave me a scare," he rumbled.

I rose up and looked him in the eye. It was the light-haired warrior from the abbey, looking tired and more wild.

His hair was longer, his light beard gnarled and matted. But it was him. Svein.

I touched his face.

He turned his head and nipped my fingers, then drew them into his mouth. "You should've at least wrapped your hands. I was afraid you'd lose a finger. You were so cold."

I lay back down, nestling into him.

"I would not have found you, if not for your hair. Like fire in the snow. Bright as a robin's breast." He tugged a few locks, then smoothed them down. His body curled tighter around me. "Miss me?"

I nodded.

"You should not have come. We've been banished, Dagg and I. I don't suppose you're here to tell us the Alphas have given us pardon?"

I shook my head.

"I didn't think so." He sounded so weary, so different from the laughing warrior who'd carried me from the abbey. He's always been more light-hearted of the pair.

Where was Dagg? Even as I thought, a howl broke out. It came from close by.

I raised my head and peered into the thicket.

"He'll not come close to the fire. His mind is gone. I'm sorry, lass." Svein kept stroking my hair as if to bring me comfort. Something told me he did it to comfort himself as well. "If you wanted to see my warrior brother, you've come too late."

15

J uliet

MORNINGS in the lodge of unmated spaewives were much like ones in the abbey. As a former orphan turned nun, I'd often been tasked with watching over the abbey's young charges. Only now I had giant, hulking Berserker warriors monitoring my every move, instead of the Mother Superior.

It was day three of the bad blizzard, and the girls were restless.

"I'm bored," Meadow flopped on her bed, rumpling her dress. I bit my tongue.

"Can we walk to Laurel's?" Violet asked.

"No, sweetheart," I lifted her and set her beside Meadow. "It's snowing too hard. Perhaps if you ask nicely, Meadow will plait your hair."

"She needs a wash first," Meadow said, but dutifully sat

up and started piecing out strands of the younger girl's hair to braid.

"Yes, when can we wash?" Rosalind spoke up. She sat in the corner with her sister, Aspen. The two blonde girls were as prim and still as dolls. Aspen's plaits were perfect.

"When the snow melts, dummy," Meadow said.

"Meadow," I chastised her. "We can fetch snow and melt it in a tub."

"Why don't we make the warrior's do it?" Rosalind asked. "They are eager to help. Especially you, Juliet."

I paused, trying to detect any bitterness in Rosalind's voice. She was a prickly one.

"I'd rather not impose on our guards," I said.

"Why not?" Meadow asked. "They'd love to please you. Especially Jarl and—"

"They have more important things to attend to," I spoke firmly, and rose and went to the hearth. Hopefully setting my back to the room would end the matter. The less I asked of the warriors, the better. I did not want to draw attention to myself.

So far no one had noticed my absences. It was only a matter of time before the secret got out, and then everyone would know I suffered the spaewife fever.

"It's not fair," Meadow muttered. "Sage and Willow and the others come and go as they please, and we're stuck in here."

"Our friends don't go as they please," Rosalind argued. "They are mated." The twist of her mouth told the room she thought this was a fate worse than death, or slavery.

Meadow shrugged. "They have warriors who care for them and see to their every need. How is that so bad?"

"Perhaps you should go entice the warriors to draw you

a bath. You seem eager to have one claim you," Rosalind sniffed.

"Enough." I turned from the hearth. "Meadow, finish Violet's hair. The rest of us will tidy up the lodge. I'll see about getting snow for washing."

"Curse this blizzard and this lodge," Meadow grumbled. "I would be glad to mate a warrior if I could only leave."

"You could always sneak out at night," Rosalind suggested. My skin prickled, and when I turned the older blonde sister was looking straight at me.

"I wouldn't advise that," I said cooly. "Who knows what dangerous beasts lurk on this mountain?" Inside, I was shaking. Did Rosalind know my secret? Would she tell?

"Did you send anyone to Laurel's for bread this morning?" Violet cut in.

"No," I said, and stilled as the young girl pointed to an empty bed.

"Then where's Fern?"

16

F ern

SVEIN AND I LAY CLOSE, watching the snow fall. He'd found a rocky ledge and tucked us under the overhang. His great body warmed me through and through.

"Blizzard will be over soon, and then I'll move you to better shelter," he muttered. "It's been a hard winter. It's not good for you to be out in these elements." His voice was deep and soothing, but sad. "You should not have come."

I bit my lip. When the blizzard was over, would he send me back? I rolled to face him. Golden eyes burned out of a lean face. His beard was wild, but he didn't look like a madman. Just tired. Perhaps a bit annoyed. He didn't want me here, where he felt he couldn't care for me.

Bowing my head, I pressed myself to his chest. I had to come up with a way to convince him to keep me as his mate.

In the meantime, I would sleep. For the first time in

weeks, I did not worry about nightmares. My warriors would keep them away, as they had before.

After a long stretch of unbroken rest, I woke to Svein's voice calling from far away.

"Wake up, little one. You must eat."

He held a hand to my lips and cold water trickled into my mouth. Melted snow. I accepted a drink and a bit of hard bread, then Svein bundled me up and lifted me easily as a sack of dandelion fluff. He carried me across a blinding white landscape. Through a gap in the furs, I looked around for his warrior brother, but Dagg was nowhere in sight.

Svein must've noticed me searching. "He's lost to us. The beast has taken over his mind."

I let my head rest back on Svein's hard chest. I'd waited too long. If Svein was right, I'd never see Dagg again. My heart ached.

Svein ducked under a rocky overhang and crawled into a cave. He set me a few feet inside, and even though I was still wrapped in the cloak, I shivered.

"Wait here," he said. "I must build a fire for you. You're too cold, and too small by half to be out in this weather."

I huddled in the place he left me, staring blindly at the wintery world. A shape moved in the woods. An animal? Or something else?

I didn't relax until Svein returned. He built the fire, and even took a branch and knocked away all the cobwebs in the corner of the cave. Once the blaze burned high, he sat and pulled me into his lap.

"Why did you come, Fern? Why are you here?"

I licked my lips. The wind blew up harder, whipping the fire until sparks flew. He held out a hand to shield me from them and cursed when I shivered.

"You should not be here. It's not safe for you."

A howl broke from the woods. I rose but Svein tugged me down.

"No. You cannot save him. It's not safe."

I stared at him. The Dagg I knew would never, ever hurt me.

"I see what you are thinking, little one, and it will not work. He is lost. Promise me you will give him up."

Instead I busied myself examining Svein. His face was lined, and his beard was almost as long as Dagg's had been. He wore a leather jerkin and breeches, thin protection against the cold. He'd wrapped all his pelts around me.

There was a dark stain on the side of his jerkin, near where it was ripped. Frowning, I followed the tear to his back, where the garment gaped open. There was blood on his skin, black flakes caked against the leather. I tugged at the shirt and Svein sighed.

"You wish to see what Dagg has become? Here." He stripped off the jerkin and showed me the wounds, long angry cuts made by a giant claw. "Got these days ago, before the blizzard."

With a whimper of sympathy, I touched his skin. The wounds were red and raw, but that could not be right. Berserkers healed faster than that.

"We've been fighting, little one."

I stared at him. Warrior brothers shared a bond closer than any other except for the mating bond. Dagg would not fight Svein unless the curse had driven him from his mind.

"He is Dagg no longer, but a monster."

I kept examining the wound until Svein shook me off.

"Don't fuss over me, lass. You should be thinking of yourself."

Pursing my lips into a stubborn expression, I came to him with one of the pelts and wrapped it around his shoulder. He gazed at me sadly. "I can't believe you came. First the bread, and now..."

Shivering, I stepped close and waited before him. His arms came around me, and I sagged against his chest. His head rested on mine. "You should have left us for dead. We are beyond saving."

I raised my head and he put a finger to my lips to stop me from protesting.

"We've been driven from our pack. They have cut us off from their presence. We heal slower now, if we heal at all."

I held him tighter.

"It's no use," he went on murmuring almost to himself. "The end will be soon. We will spiral quickly into madness."

Almost violently, I wrenched myself from his arms. I went to my bag, where I'd packed a little cup. I filled it with snow and set it near the fire to melt. Svein sat and watched me. The pelt hung loose about his shoulders, but even bare-chested he didn't seem to notice the cold.

I poured water over the wounds to clean them and bound his side with strips torn from my gown.

"You should not care for me, lass," he muttered.

I squeezed his hand.

"I'll have to return you to the Alphas."

I shook my head frantically. He rose, and I held onto him, pushing up onto my tiptoes to twine my arms around his neck. My ear rested on his chest, over his heart beat. At last his arms came around me. His hands slid over my back.

"Why did you come?" he asked again. "Did something happen?" When I didn't answer, he tipped my chin up.

I pressed my lips together. *Don't speak. Don't speak.*

He must have seen the stricken look on my face because he shook his head. "Never mind. You always were a quiet one. Come," he coaxed me near the blaze, and made me eat more bread. "You don't have enough weight on you to last the winter."

I broke the roll in half and thrust it into his hands. He was thinner too, stripped to muscle with nothing to spare. Still big, though. He towered over me.

I would not stand long against him, if he eventually did lose his mind.

"I need to hunt. But I dare not leave you long."

I touched his shoulder, leaning into him. His arms came around me, and I relaxed. More than food, I was hungry for his touch.

"I'm glad you came. Even if you should not have. You put yourself in grave danger," he growled, and this time I touched his lips to stop his protest. When I could bring myself to speak, I would tell him there was no safe place for me outside the shelter of his arms.

17

J uliet

ALL DAY, the girls sat in small pockets about the lodge, whispering. I quelled their talk as much as I could, but eventually one of the Berserkers would come and find out.

As if conjured by my thoughts, Jarl appeared with more wood for the fire. I kept away, pretending to be busy with some mending, but after a few minutes the lodge fell silent, and the shadow of the big warrior fell across my hands.

"Come with me." Jarl was frowning.

With a sigh, I followed him around the hearth where we would not be seen. It was colder here, by the door. Normally Jarl would notice me shivering and fetch a pelt for me. This time he waited for me to speak first and growled when I did not.

"One of your friends is missing."

Wrapping my arms around myself, I shrugged.

"She won't survive long in this blizzard. Tell me where she has gone."

A scrape of the door told me another had joined us. Fenrir, the only warrior I'd met who was taller than Jarl. He moved to occupy the small space between the door and the hearth with us, and despite my promise to myself not to be intimidated, I took a step back.

"I don't know where she went. She wasn't here this morning."

Jarl cursed. "Then we must find her quickly."

"It was her choice to leave." Rage bubbled up suddenly. Who were these warriors to storm into our home and take us, and keep us like pets?

I started to stomp past Jarl and he caught my arm.

"Juliet—"

"Don't touch me," I hissed. Instantly his hand fell away.

"Juliet," he repeated, but Fenrir, his warrior brother, made a signal and Jarl fell silent. One untoward move, and I could report these warriors to the Alphas. They'd never be allowed close to me again, if they were allowed to live.

"We have to tell the Alphas," he repeated. "She could be in danger." He ran a hand through his hair. "Why would she leave?"

"The wolves," Rosalind said. The blonde girl stood by the hearth, her eyes spitting sparks.

"What?"

"The missing ones. Fern knew them. The warriors took her from them before you brought her to the mountain."

"That's not..." Jarl trailed off, shaking his head. "I heard stories..."

"I was there," Rosalind said sharply. "She tried to stay with them, even when they were raving like animals."

"What happened?" I asked.

"The Corpse King attacked them, and their minds were lost," Jarl said, his gaze faraway. "The Alphas ordered them driven off the mountain."

"It's their howls we hear at night," Rosalind said. "They stay as close to her as they can."

"That's what Fern did, then," I said. "She returned to her lost mates."

18

F ern

NIGHT FELL and Svein kept the fire burning high. He went out into the snow again and again, returning with more sticks and logs for the fire, enough to last us until morning.

I was half asleep when a long lonely note broke out from the woods. Dagg's howl filled the world, sad and achingly lovely.

Svein growled and pulled me further into the shadows at the back of cave, placing himself between me and the sound.

"Svein," my hands sought him in the darkness. I found his face and held it. "He is not the enemy. He is your warrior brother."

"Not anymore."

"We must help him," I whispered.

Svein's fingers bit into my skin, but he stopped growling.

Finally, the howling stopped. Svein fetched the pelts from near the fire and built a bed for us in the depths of the cave. He pulled me down to him and wrapped his arms and legs around me. We lay in silence for a time.

"I had not heard your voice in a long time." He tugged a lock of my hair. "Little red."

"Fern," I said. "My name is Fern."

"You remember us?"

"Dagg and Svein."

"We took you from the abbey and spent a day together on the run."

"Three days," I corrected. I turned to face him. His body was hard under mine. Every once and a while, a tremor went through him. Not weakness, though. Longing. My own body pulsed in answer.

I did not know how it was possible to miss someone I'd known only a few days out of a life spent apart.

"You came to find me," Svein murmured. Perhaps he was wondering the same thing I was. "You do not remember our crimes." His mouth tugged a rueful smile. "You do not remember the night the Corpse King attacked?"

I shook my head.

"Very well little one." He settled me. "I will tell you."

19

S *vein*

THEN

THE LITTLE RED-HAIRED one lay in my arms. *She did not speak but looked about with wide eyes. As soon as we caught her scent, we'd known she was for us. We had promised not to frighten or rush her, but to woo her slowly. Above all, we would remember our honor.*

Besides, it was no great hardship to hold such a beautiful creature, to speak softly to her and feed her from our hands. By the time we reached the mountain, we would have her trained to our touch.

Even now she looked about boldly, and when Dagg offered her meat she did not flinch or shy away. I stroked her hair as she ate, reveling in the shining locks, the fiery color of leaves in the fall. She was a shy thing, used to hiding. When the mist claimed us she'd been so afraid, trembling. It took a half day to coax her from that place of terror.

"Soon we will be home," Dagg told her. "We've built a lodge to live in. It's been a long time since we've had one, but it is time. We are looking forward to staying there, with our mate."

"We will have to get used to doing chores," I said. "Chopping wood for the fire. Hunting for meat to feed our mate. Tilling the land for her to sow seeds." I sifted my fingers through her hair. We had not told her yet that we intended to claim her as mate.

"Yes," Dagg said. "Perhaps we should cut a window in the lodge wall."

"A window?"

"Our mate might want to see the outside."

"What do you think, little red?" I asked, turning the girl's face to mine.

She bit her lip and nodded.

Dagg smiled. "A window it is. Finish your meat. The sooner we leave, the sooner you will see your new home." He rose to scout ahead and returned. "The mist is clearing. We should go."

We took turns carrying our red-haired captive. Not once did her feet touch the ground.

When my turn came again, I hitched her closer and she grabbed my cloak with her small hands. She was so tiny and precious, I marveled that we'd been blessed with such a gift.

The way grew dark, the mist swirled. Our little dove whimpered.

"Do not fear," I murmured into her hair. "We will keep you safe always."

As soon as I made the promise, a horrible sound broke in the distance.

I ducked behind a boulder, holding the shivering woman close.

"Some of the pack is ahead," Dagg reported. "They're being attacked." He drew his weapon. "Run."

I ran, my treasured bundle held tight in my arms. Branches scraped at us and I did my best to shield her. The monster within fought to burst from my flesh. I gritted my teeth against the Change.

Foul winds swept over the earth. Draugr poured from the trees—the risen dead, animated by magic to walk as servants of the Corpse King.

The monster was close now. It was hard to hold back. Only the woman kept the beast at bay.

Ahead, Dagg roared. I could wait no longer. I boosted the woman into a tree and ran to the fray, slashing the corpses, laughing wildly with battle lust. The beast longed for blood even as my stomach churned at the draugr's stench and the sick taste of their rotting flesh.

Ahead were a group of Berserkers fighting. They stood in a circle, protecting their women in the center as the corpse soldiers pressed in. Dagg and I stood back to back, routing and fighting the enemy.

The woman stood on a high branch, safe from any undead hands. We were almost to the other Berserkers side when a skeleton appeared, riding the mist and wind. "He's directing the storm!" Dagg snarled at the Corpse King made flesh.

The ground rippled as bones flew from the earth, knitting together with terrible magic. More draugr formed in midair, malformed shapes that could not possibly move except as the living dead.

The woman screamed. One of the Corpse King's servants stood shaking the tree where she hid. I could not stop the monster bursting from my skin.

The Berserker rage claimed my mind and I knew nothing, felt nothing, saw nothing but red.

.   .   .

***

DAGG

RED. Everything red and shadow. A blood tinged world I cannot escape. Something moves in the darkness, lumbering and snuffing on the hunt. A monster lurking in the dark. That is what I've become.

A light pierces my world. A fire in a cave. The beast doesn't want to get close. I barely remember when I sat at a fire and conversed like a man. That life is long gone now, the humanity I had, a dream.

And yet I find myself close to the cave. Two voices, one high, one deep. I push closer as the branches part. A scent waits for me, dancing on the snow, delicate. A woman. Her voice coos like a dove.

Memory tugs and I stop in my tracks. Once I held a woman in my arms. She was fragile and silent. My salvation. But then the monster came and used my hands to almost rip her apart...

The howl tears from my throat as I remember what I have done. What I have become.

20

F ern

THE HOWLING STARTED AGAIN JUST as Svein finished his tale.

"Dagg attacked the Berserkers and threatened the women. His mind was lost. I was too far gone myself to pull him back. We were driven off, not allowed to see you again, or gain entrance to the pack's mountain."

"But... Dagg fought the Corpse King's men too. He rescued us."

"He fought everyone," Svein corrected gently. "He even swiped at you when you approached to calm him. You don't remember?"

I shook my head. The mist, the stench, the Corpse King's fighters—it was all a blur. A waking vision. I was not worried at the time because I had two strong warriors to care for me. When I woke later, and a strange warrior was carrying me, that was when I panicked. They'd taken me to the lodge of unmated spaewives, and finally told me I had no mates. That was when the dreams started again.

"He tried to attack you. When the Alphas found out, they drove him away."

I bit my lip. His banishment was my fault. "Please, we must tell them he didn't mean it."

"He said you bore the scent of the Corpse King," Svein shook his head. "He made no sense. He has lost his mind. I am sorry, Fern."

I pressed myself against his strong chest, wondering how it could be that I came so far and still felt that all was lost.

"I must ask again, little one. Why are you here?"

I drew in a long breath. "I need you."

Frowning, he cocked his head to the side. "Were you're not well cared for?"

"No, I was, but I cannot stay there." I ducked my head. How can I explain that when I was with them, I did not dream? The visions did not claim me, and I was finally safe.

"I must send you back."

"No. Please do not send me away."

He raised a brow, waiting for my reason. I thought frantically. "They will punish me."

His mouth tipped. "Do you think I will not punish you for risking your life in the blizzard?"

My heartbeat stuttered in my chest.

"Don't look so shocked, little one. I half jest. I would never harm you. Not truly. Any punishment I give will be for your benefit, and mine."

I looked at him curiously then, no longer afraid.

He stared out of the cave into the night. The trees were shrouded in white. No more snow fell, but when the wind picked up flakes and sent them swirling. "The monster beats at my skin, but with you here, I am whole. How many decades did I long for one such as you?"

I took out the last of the bread and offered it to him.

He shook his head. "Tomorrow I will hunt."

21

F ern

THE HOWLING CONTINUED LONG into the night. I lay in Svein's arms, listening. Dagg sounded like a wounded animal.

What would I do if it was too late? If their minds were truly lost? I had come so far and risked too much to fail them.

"Get on with you," Svein raised his head and called into the darkness. "She's not for you, or me. Not anymore." His body was tense as he lay back down. "Don't cry, little one." He said to me. "It will be all right."

Nodding against his chest, I swiped the tears from my cheeks. Svein smelled of snow, and wood smoke, and damp fur. Solid scents that comforted me. My legs tangled with his, and the heat from his body warmed me.

But Dagg was still out there, howling in the snow, alone. Even when the sound stopped, I stayed awake a long time.

Svein woke me with a kiss on the lips. He was up and naked but for a pelt around his hips. Morning light slanted through the cave.

"I'll be back soon. Stay here, and do not leave the cave."

I huddled in the furs and dozed. Svein had built up the fire before he left, and I watched it slowly dwindle to ash. I should rise and add a log to it, but the pelts were just too warm. When the last sparks glowed deep in the charred depths, I sat up, then froze.

Beyond the mouth of the cave, near the bushes, the shadows moved. A large creature with dark, matted fur and glowing eyes lurked there. It kept hidden, sniffing and shuffling closer.

I was on my feet in a second. "Dagg?"

No answer, but the creature moved halfway into the light. A hunched monster, taller than any man, with the furry muzzle, paws and claws of a beast, came into view.

A growl made us both turn. A white wolf stood at the forest edge, teeth bared.

"Svein, no," I cried, too late. The monster took a few steps back but didn't escape before the wolf attacked. Snow flew. I shouted and waved my hands for them to stop, wincing as the wolf's jaw clamped down on the monster's arm. The monster rose on its hind legs, vicious claws raking at the great wolf's back. Blood flew into the snow.

"Stop!" I picked up a log stacked by the fire and threw it. It bounced off the two of them. They broke apart for a moment, the monster staggering backwards. The wolf lunged for it again.

"No," I shrieked. "Svein, it's Dagg! It's Dagg—don't hurt him."

Rearing back, the monster beat a retreat to the trees. The wolf remained, lips peeled back, muzzle streaked with blood. As I watched, its forelegs pushed off the ground, and the beast rose to its back legs, shaking off fur and turning into a man. My hair blew back with a sudden wind.

Svein stalked back into the cave, still moving with the lean grace of a wild animal. I rushed at him and pushed at his chest. "What did you do?"

Svein blinked in surprise. Blood trickled from his back and a cut on his face. More wounds from a stupid, useless fight. "Didn't you see?"

His growl cut off, his golden eyes searching my face. I realized I'd never raised my voice before.

"Did he hurt you?" Svein ground out. His eyes were bright and wild. The battle lust was still upon him.

I shook my head and held still as his hands roamed over me, reassuring himself I was whole. He sniffed my hair.

"Svein," I whispered, and he pulled me into his embrace.

"Forgive me. I shouldn't have left you alone."

"It's not that." I pushed away from him. "He did not want to fight you."

"Little one…"

"I saw it. I was right here." I thumped his bare chest.

Svein stood thinking. "What did he do?" He asked at last.

"Nothing. He came up to the cave, and waited there, sniffing the air."

"He scented you."

"Perhaps. But he did not venture in, even though I let the fire go out."

"I never should've left you alone." Shaking his head, Svein went to build up the fire.

"You had to. We need to eat."

When he was done, he rose, dusting off his hands, and went to the clothes he'd left stacked neatly for when he returned from the hunt. I stopped him long enough to wipe the blood from his cuts. His eyes swept over me hungrily. According to the stories my mated friends told, the beast did not only lust for blood. I kept my eyes downcast and shook a little as I stepped away.

I ventured out of the cave to fetch some water and stopped. "Svein, come look."

A bloody bundle lay under the bushes. A hank of meat, the fur still clinging to it. "He left a kill."

Svein came and pushed me gently back to the cave. He sniffed the meat carefully. "Deer."

"Don't you see? He brought this here."

"Good, because my hunt was futile. The prey in these woods are in hiding, frightened of Dagg's monster."

I huffed. "He's not a monster."

"What else would you call that thing?" Svein squatted in the snow to skin the meat and fetched some branches. In no time he had made a spit and my stomach was gurgling with the scent of roasting meat.

We ate well, thanks to Dagg. Svein let me fill my belly and devoured the rest, licking juice from his fingers.

"More snow tonight."

I shivered. Dagg was out there, alone.

Svein stalked over with a pelt and wrapped it around me. His touch was so gentle, as if I was fragile and might fall apart.

"You need to go back, Fern. I cannot care for you."

I knotted my forehead. "I did not come only for you to care for me. I came to rescue you."

"You assume we can be rescued."

"You are of sound mind."

"Perhaps. For now."

I bit my lip. I wanted so much to save these men, the

only ones who could save me. "Does it help for me to be here?"

"Yes, it helps." he admitted. "But I don't know how long it will last."

"It will last." It had to.

Svein smiled as if my vow amused him. He tossed the meat bones out into the snow and built up the fire again.

Large shadows danced on the walls as I looked about the cave. This would be our home at least until the biggest snow drifts melted. When the Berserkers first took me, they spoken of a lodge they'd built for their mate. I'd dreamed of it. But for now, this cave would do.

Rising, I took off my cloak.

"I wish to bathe," I said. Svein raised a brow. I took a scrap of cloth from my bag and a cup I'd brought. Once the water had warmed, I washed as best I could, wiping down my face and neck and running the rag underneath my gown. Svein watched with great interest, to the point where when it came time to wash my legs, I blushed and turned away.

I stood by the fire to dry, then dumped the water out of the cup and refilled it.

"Your turn." Svein looked amused again, and it heartened me to see more of a smile on his tired face. Heat leapt between his body and mine, and I could not stop blushing. I focused instead on wiping the dirt from his face and neck. At my request he stripped off his jerkin and bent so I could wash his hair.

"Of all the punishments I could devise, cleaning my dirty self is the worst," he chuckled.

Watching the clean water run down his sculpted chest, I could not agree. I did not understand the magic in him, any more than I understood my own dreadful visions. But there was something between us, growing in the most unlikely place, a flower blossoming between a rock.

I set the cloth aside and splayed a hand against his hard chest. He sucked in a breath but didn't move away. Leaning forward, I pressed a kiss to his collarbone.

A howl rang out, faint and faraway, from somewhere deep in the forest.

I startled back. Svein's mouth curved ruefully, but he didn't pursue me.

"Do you think Dagg is hurt?"

"It does not matter, little dove. He will not come near the fire."

"You must try to find him," I said, and ripped my sleeve. "Take this. It bears my scent."

"I cannot leave you defenseless," he choked.

"Take it. Go. I will stay by the fire. As you said, he will not come close. But we must lure him here."

"You mean it."

"I did not come so that he could die. I came to save you both," I poked the fire.

"Very well." he rose. He looked stronger, his cheeks and eyes less sunken. His face healthy in the firelight. "I will return." He walked to the edge of the cave and hesitated.

"I will be safe," I promised. "I will stay near the fire."

His mouth drew up in a half grin.

"We always knew you would find your voice," he said. "I am glad to hear it at last."

22

F ern

SNOW FLURRIES FILLED the air by the time Svein returned. I'd kept the fire burning high, using the stack of wood he'd left and not venturing one step beyond the cave. As soon as his blond head came into view, I rose to greet him.

He grinned and raised his arm, showing me the rabbits in his hand.

"Oh, well done," I breathed. His grin widened.

To my surprise, he advanced, locked his free arm around me, and caught my mouth in a kiss. Warmth shot straight to my toes, pooling at my center.

I broke away to ask, "Dagg?"

Svein jerked a head back the way he came. "There, by the rock."

I had to look hard to distinguish the large dark wolf from the shadows at the edge of the forest. But it was him.

"He came. And in wolf form. But how—"

"No time to explain. Storm is coming, worse than the last. We must make ready."

Svein set me skinning the rabbits while he fetched more wood. I fed the fire as he built a lean-to to shield the cave from the worst of the wind. Dagg, still in wolf form, hovered just in sight. Pretending to look for kindling, I found the old bones from our last meal, and flung them in his direction. When I turned, Svein was watching me, brows raised. I washed my hands in the snow and refused comment. But I sensed he wasn't altogether displeased. Dagg was with us, and in wolf form. Whatever grip the Berserker curse had on him had weakened.

Svein flung a new pelt down and sat. He spitted the rabbits and cooked them. The dark wolf came closer, and we pretended not to notice. When we were done with our meal, I crept to the edge of the cave and held out my hand with the rabbit carcass.

"Careful," Svein muttered.

"It's Dagg," I reminded him and myself. Not a strange wolf, not a monster. Dagg looked so dark and serious, but he had been kind and playful too. Not as playful as Svein, who'd often smiled. Tonight, Svein just looked tired.

I tossed the bones close to the wolf and returned to Svein's side. I drew the warrior to the bed of pelts and pulled him down, tucking myself under his arm. The wind howled outside, loud as a wolf, but here in the cave we were safe in a pocket of warmth.

"Sleep," I told him.

"I must keep watch."

I raised my head to look for the wolf. Sure enough, the dark head was half in darkness, half in firelight as it worried the bone between its paws. He'd come right up to the lean-to entrance, lying between us and the wind. "Dagg will do it."

Svein must have been too tired to argue, for he rolled over and folded me in his arms. I tucked my hands under his jerkin, resting my palms against the warm flesh. I wriggled a little to get comfortable and his cock grew against me.

"Careful," he half growled.

I paused, then let my hand wander, finding the gap between his jerkin and breeches. His body tensed.

"Fern," Svein rasped in my ear, "you must know what you do to me."

I grew bolder, slipping my hand lower until it circled around his cock.

My cheeks heated but I met his golden gaze.

"I want—"

He dipped his head and claimed my mouth. His beard scraped my chin, but his lips were warm, pulling on mine, coaxing and claiming. He grew even larger and harder in my hand.

I whimpered, shifting my hips. He shucked down his jerkin enough to free himself. "Do what you will, little red. I am yours."

I slid my fingers up and down, jacking him slowly. Fluid leaked from the tip. His flesh seemed so red and angry, throbbing under my touch.

"Does it hurt?"

Svein buried his face in my hair. "The scent of you is enough to drive a man mad. With desire, not rage."

"I want to be with you," I whispered. "Please let me stay."

After a pause, he nodded.

"If it is safe, you may stay with us."

I relaxed against him. The battle was won. Now for the war.

But first I would please my mate. I licked my palm and closed my slick hand around him again. His ragged breathing guided me, told me where to touch and stroke, when to squeeze and when to be gentle. His shaft seemed to swell in size, and I felt he was close to spending when he stopped me. His mouth found mine and kissed me into a daze. Need bloomed in me, so strong I forgot what I was doing.

A chuckle broke from him. "You act so shy, but you are fierce as a warrior. A wolf on the hunt."

"Are you my prey?"

"No," he said against my mouth, and rolled so I was under him, my hand still stroking him slowly. "You are mine."

His mouth came to my neck and I gasped, arching up at the sensation shooting through me. With little nips and pulls, he worried my neck until it was aching and tender.

"When the time comes, we will mark our mate. She will have to be very brave and strong to hold the beast at bay."

I bared my teeth at him and he chuckled.

"But soft, and sweet. She will quicken to our touch," I sucked in a breath as his own hand went beneath my gown. "Just as we will ache under hers."

"Do you ache for me then?"

"Every night. Every night."

He moved and suddenly our bodies were in tune, working together against each other's hands.

"Soon I will put my mouth on you, and make you scream into the night. You will find pleasure again and again, until you don't remember your name."

"Svein," I whispered, jerking a little as sensation flooded through me.

"That's it, take your pleasure."

He rose up over me, watching me writhe. His fingers kept at it, sending little whips of pleasure through my shaking body. His eyes took in every movement, every moan, every expression.

"And now," he drew out his cock and pushed up my gown, "You will wear my scent."

He took himself in hand and tugged faster, frowning with concentration. I could only lay there, sleepy and heavy with satisfaction, as he spurted his seed on my thighs, marking me thoroughly.

"Fern," he breathed and came back down to lie with me, curling his large body around mine. Within seconds he was asleep.

Before I let myself do the same, I craned my head. The wolf stood at the entrance of the cave, facing the wind. He would not join us this night as a man.

But soon, I promised myself. *Soon.*

23

F^{ern}

"FOR YEARS we stayed in *Norvergr*, fighting for Harald Fairhair. Twenty or thirty summers, I think." Svein glanced at the wolf who waited outside as if looking for confirmation.

I sat near the fire, watching the snowfall, half listening to Svein continue his story.

"Then we boarded dragon-headed ships and crossed the sea. There were some islands the king wanted to conquer. North of here. Do you know why they called the king 'Fairhair'?"

"Because he had blond hair?" I guessed.

"That and he refused to cut it until he conquered all he could. Some promise he made to a lady."

"Did he ever cut it?"

Svein shrugged. "He was the king. He did as he pleased."

Outside the lean-to, the wolf slumped in the snow. The blizzard had dumped more onto the already massive drifts. I wished Dagg would come in but as Svein said, he kept his distance from the fire.

"Did you like fighting for this king?"

"Wasn't a matter of like or not. We liked fighting. We were made for it."

"The witch made you." I kept my eye on the wolf, hoping our conversation would not trigger his battle lust.

"The witch turned us from men into fighting beasts, yes. Eventually we realized it was a curse. By then it was too late. We fought and conquered, year after year, until the madness claimed most of us. Some Berserkers left and followed one called Bodolf, and his son Ragnvald. Svein and I went with Sigmund, now called Samuel."

"He's the Alpha of the mountain."

"He is the most powerful of us not because of strength alone, but because his control over the beast. Even then he was almost lost to the rage, if he hadn't found his mate."

"Brenna of the Berserkers." I'd heard this story, whispered among the spaewives. She was the first of us and ruled as queen along with the Alphas. "So, it is possible for a warrior to be almost lost, and to return to himself."

"It is not common, but perhaps it can be done."

After a while the snow abated. Svein disappeared for a time and I dozed in the pelts, tossing and turning. Dagg's shadow fell across the cave mouth, his wolf caught between the wilderness and his place by the fire. He was waiting, always waiting, but I slept as if he guarded my dreams. I hadn't had a vision since I'd come to them. My dreams were full of shadows, but safe from the specter who'd haunted them before. He could not reach me with Dagg and Svein here. With that comforting thought, I slipped into sleep.

When I woke, it was snowing again. Svein had returned holding a large stew pot. He filled it with snow and set it on the fire and added wood until the water simmered.

"There," he said when I sat up. "You said you wanted to bathe."

"Where did you...?" My voice trailed off. He'd gone somewhere and snatched the pot. I didn't need to know where. Instead, I added some herbs to the fire and asked him to move the pot off the blaze. He raised a brow but did as I bid.

"A strange broth."

"It's not for eating. I want to wash your hair." My earlier attempt hadn't been as thorough as I'd liked.

He grimaced. "Better to cut it." He took his knife and sliced through the locks, letting the ragged braid fall.

"Let me." I took the knife and evened the ends of the shorn locks. Then I had him bend so I could pour water over his head. I soaped the silky straw-colored tufts, untangling the smaller snarls, rubbing the dirt from his scalp and neck. A few cups of water poured over his head and the water ran clean.

"Much better," I murmured but kept playing with his hair. He held still, allowing my touch. Little currents of energy ran up my arms, down my body, as if I submitted to him, rather than the other way around.

I was close to cupping his face and pleading for a kiss when Svein lifted his head at some soft noise.

"What is it?"

"Wait here." He rose and strode to the mouth of the cave, drawing his weapon.

I followed until he motioned for me to stop. From what I could see of the dark, snow-filled world, the wolf was gone. "Is it..."

"Dagg. He is out there."

"As a man?" my chest tightened. "We need to invite him in."

"No. He's not... himself." Not a man then.

"I want to see him," I started forward, but Svein caught me.

"If he was in his right mind, he would not want you to see him."

A gust swept by the cave, sending flurries as far as the fire. The wolf had waited for the moment he could stand to come inside. But it had never come. Instead, he'd watched me with his warrior brother, and despaired.

"Your hair is turning to icicles," I tugged Svein back, tears in my eyes.

"It's not your fault. Fern—"

"Hold me, please," I pressed against him, hiding my face in his neck.

His arms came around me, and he let us both sink down onto the pelts.

I straddled his lap, sniffling back my tears long enough to dry his hair. Svein studied me, but I kept my gaze averted. Bowing my head, I tugged at the laces of his breeches.

"Fern—" he caught my hands.

"Please. I need you."

In one movement he laid me back under him.

"You think I would refuse you?"

I shook my head. My desire was bittersweet, knowing Dagg was most likely lost, but I still had one warrior with me. I could not deny my craving any more.

"I've dreamt of this every night," Svein rasped. His hand slipped under my clothes and I arched into his palm. "Do you know what happens to naughty ones who wander into a wolf's territory?" His eyes glinted.

I shook my head.

His lips found my ear. "They get eaten." Teeth scraped the defenseless spot behind my ear, nipped my soft lobe. I went weak all the way to my knees.

His mouth blazed a trail downward, finally nuzzling the sensitive skin of my inner thighs.

"Here," he murmured. His bristled chin scraped me, and I jumped. Pinning me with his hands, he explored further, coming to the soft nest of auburn hair. I held still best I could, frozen like prey before a predator.

"This is where I feast." He blew hot breath on my lower lips and goosebumps broke on along my body.

"Oh, Svein—"

"That's it. Call my name, loud as you like." He lowered his head and fed. Large hands gripped my jerking hips, holding me still. His tongue delved into my secret places, finding spots that sent pleasure surging through me. He ignored my hands tugging at his hair, ignored my gasps and pleas.

"Ripe as a berry, and so sweet," he said.

My body tensed like a drawn bow, quivering with readiness. He stabbed me with his tongue, adding fingers to stretch me. I dug my heels into the ground, no longer seeking to retreat from his voracious mouth. Cries filled my ears, sounds I barely recognized as mine.

As I came back to myself, my head rolled on the pelt. Wind gusted over my face. Beyond the fire, there were eyes in the darkness, watching.

Tears leaked out of the corners of my eyes, in the face of overwhelming pleasure.

Svein was finishing, drawing out my pleasure with little cat licks and kisses. A shuddering sigh went through me and he rose up, covering my body with his.

"Shhhh, little red. It will be all right." His weight kept me safe and still, absorbing most of the pain beating in my heart.

It was not only my pain, I must remember that. Svein would bear guilt of not being able to save his warrior brother.

"I'm sorry," I mumbled, already halfway unconscious.

Svein's lips brushed mine. "I know. Sleep."

I fought to stay awake long enough to ask, "What about you?"

He kissed me thoroughly. "Tomorrow," he promised. "Tomorrow I'll teach you to please me."

24

F ern

IN THE MORNING, we found footprints in the snow. A man had paced outside our cave and left before dawn. I made Svein take me to where they disappeared in the bracken. I did not see whether they turned back into a wolf's.

"It was him. Dagg returned."

Svein's face tightened. "If he turns again into the monster, I must drive him away."

"No, don't."

Svein had already turned away, marching back to the cave. I grabbed at his hand, but he didn't slow.

"You think you can save us?"

That stopped me in my tracks. I let Svein's hand go. "I must."

"I should send you back to the pack and the Alphas."

"There is nothing for me there."

Shaking his head, he grabbed his axe and set a log on its end to split it.

"If you send me back, I will do everything I can to return. I will not stay where you put me."

Stone-faced, the warrior sent his axe slicing through one log. Picking up the two pieces he tossed them to our pile and grabbed another log.

"Svein, did you hear me? Are you listening?" I stalked around so he could not ignore me.

He set the axe down and crossed his arms over his chest. "What made me think you were quiet?"

Smiling, I swayed closer and went on tiptoes to kiss him. I still could not reach him, so he bent to my lips. I did my best to convince him to keep me until he broke away with a sigh.

"I must hunt."

"Will you keep look out for Dagg?"

He touched a finger to my lips but did not tell me to be quiet. "I expect I'll find him, if he wants to be found."

Fern

To my disappointment, he did not find Dagg that day, or the next. The snows stopped for a time, though the world stayed quiet, with all its creatures abed.

Svein and I passed the time easily in our cave. I'd brought a cup, some bread, the clothes on my back, my cloak, and boots. A few extra clothes, small packets of herbs and a bit of soap. I didn't have many possessions, but these few supplies would help me make our camp a home.

Svein and I worked to make our cave cozy. Outside winter had the world in its frozen fist, but inside was safe and warm. Svein was clever with the fire, building it under a crevice in the cave ceiling so most of the smoke went up and out, while the heat stayed. We also wore coats made of fur —every time he left to hunt, he returned with a white pelt that smelled of winter.

I cleared the last of the cobwebs and brush and piled the furs on the large flat rock that made our bed, scattering lavender from my pack around it. I kept water heated over the fire, using wintergreen leaves to make a soothing tea. Svein often left early and returned before I was awake with armfuls of firewood or game. His lean face filled out a little and he lost his hungry, haunted look. With each kill, I dried meat and set it aside, storing it as I would if we lived in a proper lodge.

One afternoon he returned late in the day. I greeted him with relief. He stooped and kissed me before showing me what caused the delay—a parcel of fresh bread, along with piece of honeycomb.

"Where did you get this?" I rewrapped the honey comb and licked my sticky fingers.

"Someone left the loaves on the bridge." He caught my hand and helped clean my fingers, but that did not distract me from blurting,

"You climbed the mountain? It's dangerous for you to go so close to the pack."

He shrugged. "They will not catch me. But you need to eat, little red. You're already too small."

"Not anymore." My own body had grown stronger, my breasts bigger. I was not big and beautiful as Laurel, but I'd noticed my gown tight around my chest. "You feed me enough meat. I'm not used to eating so much."

"You're so little. You need more food to withstand this cold." His own cheeks were ruddy from the wind as he stoked up the fire.

"You keep me warm," I reminded him, and was rewarded with a flash of heat in his eyes.

We ate the bread with honey and began our evening ritual. Every night I insisted we bathe—or clean each other as much as we could with just a little warm water and a soapy cloth--before we sank onto the furs to enjoy the comfort of each other's arms. I wetted the scrap of linen and scrubbed around Svein's neck and ears, rinsing it and swiping the soap for a little lather. His blond hair grew dark with damp as he bent his head and submitted to my ministrations. Concentrating as I was, I didn't notice his grin right away, not until he nuzzled my neck.

"Your turn," he murmured.

"Not yet." I swatted him with the cloth.

When he raised his head, his eyes blazed gold. In one movement, he pulled me down and under him. I sprawled on a pelt, eyes wide as he took the cloth. Straddling me, he tugged down the neck of my gown.

I made a noise, afraid he'd tear it.

"I'll find you another," he promised, but stopped short of ripping the garment off. The wet cloth had cooled; as he ran it along my collarbone, my nipples hardened. Carefully he rubbed around my neck and behind my ears and moved away. I started to rise, but he returned, having rewet the cloth.

"I'm clean," I said but let him lay me out again.

"Not yet," he drew up my skirts. His smile turning serious, he washed up my legs in slow swirls that set my core throbbing. He rinsed the rag again and returned, kneeling right between my legs so I had to set my knees far apart.

"What are you doing?"

"I have been a poor teacher, if we've been together so long and you don't know."

"We weren't together so long."

"Long enough for you to know to whom you belong." his gaze heated me. "Long enough for your body to know its master."

He laid the hot, damp cloth right on the thatch of red curls at the apex of my thighs. I sucked in a breath. My body tightened, quickened, a taut bowstring ready to be plucked. With a wicked look, he cleaned me carefully, taking his time tracing my lower lips and dipping into the folds.

"One day, I will shave you."

My eyes widened.

He arched a brow. "Would you like that, little red?"

"I... ohhh..."

Cupping my pussy, he slid a finger inside me. My body clenched, and my hips came off the pelts. Svein explored me with a lazy finger, his touch no more than a tickling whisper that made me long for more. "Does not matter what you wish," he commented. "You will submit to my desires. I will shave your sweet cunny and keep it as I wish." He pulled out his slick finger and licked it. "Delicious."

I whimpered.

Tossing the cloth away, he stretched out over me, finding my lips. I caught a taste of myself, a wild, earthy essence, and when Svein drew away I realized I'd been rocking my hips toward him, seeking more stimulation.

"Such a pretty wanton you are."

"I am not wanton."

"For me. Only for me." His lips caressed my neck, down my shoulders, across my neck. "A flower growing quiet under the snows. You melt only for me."

And Dagg, I wanted to add, but he claimed my mouth and I forgot anything else.

The wind picked up, Svein drew the furs over us. On one of his raids, he'd brought back a large bear robe, and I'd sewn a blanket to it, making a large pocket we could slip into. My legs tangled with his, my body twining around his great one.

He set his knee between my legs and rocked it back and forth, pushing me closer to the edge.

"Svein," I gasped.

"That's it, little red. Take your pleasure."

I gasped as sensation rushed through me. My body bucked against his leg. Panting, I clutched at him.

"Good girl," he murmured, stroking my neck as I came back down.

"I left you wet," I told him and hid my face in his chest.

"It's all right," he chuckled. "I enjoy wearing your scent. And I will mark you with mine."

"Tonight?"

"You need your sleep," He kissed me again, and settled me in his arms.

The fire crackled, and I raised my head enough to see the dark head of a wolf at the mouth of the cave.

Satisfied, I lay back down. Dagg had started to spend the nights here. He kept the shape of a wolf, but I imagined each night he came a little closer to the fire.

I fell asleep with a smile on my face, and my body warm in Svein's arms. My sleep was deeper, more restful. My dreams were there, waiting for me beyond the veil. The skeletal specter stood in the mist and gloom, but he could not reach me. Wrapped in the warm presence of my mates, I was safe.

25

F ern

THE NEXT MORNING, I stretched out my legs, coming awake slowly. The cool air on my face and the solid warmth at my back.

The sun slanted into the cave, over the snow drifts. The snow had stopped a day or two ago. It'd been five—or was it six—days since I'd come. The cave was not the lodge originally promised me, but at least we had shelter.

The fire was low—Svein would have to replenish our wood store soon. Odd that he was still abed this late, but I would not complain. I snuggled back into his chest.

And froze as soft, thick hair tickled the back of my neck. The man behind me was not Svein. He was broader, with a long beard that scraped my bare shoulder, and a wild scent.

"Miss me, little dove?"

I jerked upright at the rough voice. Dagg lay there, a grin under his thick beard. The lines were deeper on his forehead and there were dark circles under his eyes, but it was him.

"Dagg," I breathed and scrambled to face him. He chuckled as I ran my hand down his hard body, reassuring myself with his warm skin. He was human, and he was whole.

"Fern," he murmured. I ducked my head and press my cheek against him, listening to his heart beat. His hand come up to cup the back of my head, and we rested like that.

"So small," he mused, stroking my hair. "I forgot how little you are." He tugged a lock of my hair. "So fiery. I remembered this flaming hair, even when my mind was lost."

I let out a little shuddering sigh.

"Don't cry, dear one." His hand slid along my nape and I held him tighter. "The madness is gone, for now." His voice dropped to a wondering whisper. "You're so quiet."

"Svein doesn't think so. He says I vex him." I raised my head enough to look at him. "Back at the lodge of unmated spaewives, I barely spoke."

His fingers flexed against my neck. "Why did you come?"

"I couldn't leave you," I whispered.

"Svein is right. You are safer with the pack."

I lay my head against his chest.

"I was angry with him at first. He should've sent you away. But I am glad he did not. You ease the madness. But I'm afraid I'll never be whole."

I cuddled against him. In his arms I felt safe from my own madness. My body pressed flush to his, fitting perfectly.

"I suspect neither of us will be able to send you away.

Just as well. My mind is not whole but perhaps you are the missing piece."

"Svein will not be happy I am here. He seeks to protect you from me."

"You keep me safe."

"I hope so."

I took his wrist and laid his hand on my collarbone. "Touch me, Dagg."

His cock grew against my leg. "It has been too long. I must keep control."

"Do as you will," I whispered.

His mouth fitted over mine. At first, he went slowly, almost lazily feeding on my mouth. His hand found my breast and I gasped. Shifting his weight over me, he left my mouth and worried my neck, drawing from me little whimpers and cries.

He kissed down my body, and for all his talk of me being small, he took his time. He lingered at my knee and came back up to nuzzle between my legs. His beard tickled. But when I wriggled he gripped my hips and held me still.

"Who do you belong to?" he asked, his gaze hot on mine.

"To you," I said, and moaned when he rewarded me with a hot mouth on my aching center. "Dagg," he made me pant, his teeth scraping perilously close to my vulnerable heat, his tongue wicked and darting into every part of me.

When he was done, he wrapped me in a pelt and pulled me into his lap. We sat in front of the fire, me content, him sifting fingers through my hair.

A shadow loomed in the mouth of the cave.

"Svein," I cried. "Look. Dagg has returned."

My light-haired mate nodded to his warrior brother, who rose. Both stood watching each other warily.

Dagg's bare chest still bore marks from Svein's claws, and under Svein's clothes, I knew he bore the same.

"He is returned," I repeated. "We can be together again."

Svein shrugged.

When I stood, some of Dagg's spend trickled down my leg. I ignored it and went to Svein, though my face heated to the root of my hair. His lips twisted wryly, as if he knew why I blushed. I took his hand and walked him back into the cave, near the fire. The two men faced each other, tense.

"How was your hunt?" I broke the bitter silence. None of my friends from the abbey would believe I could make conversation like this, but I felt I must ease the way.

"Well enough. I got a buck and left it to drain outside." Svein drew his axe and ran a finger along the bloody edge before using a rag and some snow to clean it. "Hunting would be better if a monster hadn't driven all the prey away."

A low growling sound filled the cave. It came from Dagg. I returned to his side and it stopped.

"You must bathe. Here, Svein brought me a cauldron to use, and I have cleansing herbs."

Dagg answered "My wolf plunged into a freezing stream for you."

I grimaced. "This will be less painful." I bustled about, making ready. When the water was warmed, I tugged at the dark-bearded warrior. "Come on. Before it gets cold."

"Perhaps Svein will get us more wood for the fire." Dagg turned a pointed look to Svein.

"I'm not leaving." The blond folded his arms over his chest.

"This is Dagg," I reproached Svein. "Your warrior brother. I'm safe with him."

Dagg touched my hair. "He remembers a time that wasn't true."

"That was the Corpse King's doing. He turned you against us."

"Even so, he must atone," Svein said. "Trust isn't easily regained."

"The curse has receded. The madness is at bay. But I will atone." Dagg knelt and took my hand. "I will atone."

Dagg stayed kneeling for me, and even then, I had to lift the cup high to pour it over his head. Svein kept guard at the mouth of the cave, arms crossed over his chest, mouth set in a grim line. He watched Dagg as Dagg had watched us for so many days. Did Svein think I betrayed him? Was the bond between them so broken, we could never again be one?

As if he heard my fearful thoughts, Dagg murmured, "There is still a bond between us. He just wishes there were not."

I swept the cleaning cloth over his broad chest, wincing at the half-healed cuts under the dark mat of hair. "You need to make peace."

"Soon, little dove." He tugged me close. "First, let me enjoy my bath."

"It's not a real bath," I whispered. He slipped a hand up my leg and heat came into my face again. I twisted a little out of reach. "I need to wash, too."

"Leave it." He raised his chin and sniffed the air, eye bright. "You should smell of me, always."

I swatted him with the wet cloth. Rucking up my shift, I started to climb into the caldron, where I could thoroughly cleanse myself.

Strong arms banded around my middle. I shrieked, but Dagg lifted me easily and carried me to the pelts. He dropped me there and I rolled, dodging him. He rose, blocking my exit with his giant body. He caught me again, by the shift, and I wriggled out of it, laughing. Another grab and we went down together. Somehow, I ended up on top.

"I'm still messy," I protested when he pulled me down and hooked a heavy leg over mine.

"No sense getting clean when I'll only get you dirty again." His deep voice was guttural as a bark, and his eyes gleamed so bright I knew the beast was near.

A long kiss later and I rubbed wantonly against his hard midriff, angling my body and sighing as I reached for relief.

"Easy," Dagg growled, and pulled a pelt over my shoulders.

Heat broke through me even as he chided, "You'll catch a chill, little dove."

"You will warm me." I twisted and reached out to Svein, who had come inside the cave, the better to watch over me. "You both will."

"Peace, brother?" Dagg called. "For her sake."

"For her sake," Svein agreed. "Peace."

I pushed off Dagg and he let me go running to Svein. Dancing up to tiptoes, I wrapped my arms around Svein's neck and rewarded him with a kiss. He took control. With fist in my hair and large hand splayed over my bottom, he walked me backward until we neared our bed. Then he turned me firmly and, with an iron arm banded around my waist, drew my hair aside and fastened his lips on my neck. A bolt of lightning shot from his lips to my core. My knees buckled, and I sagged, suspended by the arm locked around me.

"Little red," Dagg knelt before me, at the right height to take my breasts in his mouth. Svein's hand slid down my front, cupping my heat. His fingers dipped inside.

A moan shuddered through me, once, twice, again. I

writhed, pinned between two men intent on delivering delicious torment. My breasts grew full and heavy under Dagg's lips. His beard tickled me

Svein's breath was hot on my neck, finding the most sensitive spots to worry. His teeth scraped my pulse, sending primal shivers through me. Any little bit of fear dissolved and drowned in desire.

Dagg's kisses reached my cunt and I arched in Svein's hold to push into Dagg's willing mouth.

"Do you want us?" Svein caught my earlobe between his teeth and bit gently.

"Yes," I gasped. My inner muscles clenched around Svein's questing fingers. Svein's teeth traced down my neck, and I remembered what my friends had said of their warriors, how Berserkers claimed their mates. Perhaps this would be a way to link Dagg and Svein together again.

"Claim me. Mark me."

A second later, Svein set my feet on the ground. "Making demands, are we?"

"Wait—"

Svein's hand closed around my neck, angling my head to face him. "You sacrifice yourself so that I might link to Dagg?" His heated gaze was almost menacing. My pulse fluttered against his palm.

"No, I just..."

Svein turned me to face Dagg.

"What shall we do with this naughty one, who risked her life coming down the mountain to save us?" Svein asked.

"Teach her to mind. Teach her who she belongs to," Dagg answered gruffly. His mouth was stern under his great beard.

"Please, I—"

"We'll mark you, little one. But not in the way you desire."

My legs gave out and Svein caught me. "I wish to shave this." His great hand cupped between my legs.

"Not bare," Dagg frowned.

"No," Svein agreed. "I like to see a little tuft of red."

I squirmed, face hot, mortified that they would speak of this. A minute later, I was on my back, splayed comfortably on the pelts, with Dagg kneeling between my legs.

Svein produced a knife and whetstone. He tested the blade against his finger and sharpened it some more.

Dagg washed me carefully with warm water, and pressed hot cloths to the apex of my legs. When they cooled he took them away and replaced them with his mouth. My body surged up into that one point of contact, pleasure trolling slowly through me.

Then Dagg was gone and Svein took his place. Firelight glinted on metal.

"Frightened?"

I shook my head.

"You should be. We are monsters. But you did not have the sense to be afraid."

Dagg sat behind me and gathered me onto his lap. He hooked my legs on either side of his and spread me wide.

"Even in those first days, you were never really afraid," he nuzzled my ear. "That is how we knew you belonged to us."

Svein bent to his task. I shut my eyes. In some ways it was worse, being perfectly attuned to the feeling of his fingers stroking across my soap-slicked skin, the wet sound of the blade separating the red down from my flesh. Dagg kept my legs firmly apart. Svein pressed a hand above my pubic bone, holding me still. I lay perfectly open, my bones melting into Dagg's sturdy form, my body rising and falling with his breath. I had no being, no sense of myself beyond the points of where they touched me, claimed me, owned me.

And when Svein was done, they lay me down and took turns showing me how I belonged to them. I begged and begged, but they did not mark me. Not yet. But I knew they would soon.

26

F ern

"NOW THAT THE snows are less, we might have visitors." Svein commented the next morning. He squatted by the firepit, poking leaves into the ashes to see if one would light.

"Visitors?" I asked.

"Some of the pack, hunting us."

"But, the Alpha's cut you off."

"Yes," Dagg said, coming in with an armful of wood. "and there's one benefit to that. They won't be able to find us as easily."

"They can track us," Svein commented, moving out of the way so Dagg could finish the fire.

"We can hide our tracks."

"Wait," I said. "Why don't you want them to find you?"

Svein had his knife out now and was rubbing soap on his face to shave. He caught me watching and grinned. The memory of that knife sent heat flooding to my lower half, and I blushed.

"They'll take you from us again and drive us away. My guess is the snow is what kept them away so long," Dagg said.

"If they bother," Svein mused. "My guess, they won't risk this happening again. They'll call for our death."

I gasped.

"The blizzards kept them away, but now we must be careful."

"I do not want you to die," I said.

"Nor I," Dagg murmured. "Not when we found a reason to live."

Once the fire was built, and Svein tested the smoothness of his cheeks by rubbing them on my face and kissing me, both warriors rose.

"We need to go hunt." Svein strapped on his knife and axe, while Dagg studied his hand, curling his fingers inward like they were tipped with claws.

"Both of you?"

"It takes two to bring down big prey, little red." Dagg cupped the back of my neck and pulled me forward to plant a kiss on my brow. "We'll return by sundown."

"Stay in the cave," Svein ordered.

I tidied up and took the time to properly wash. I spent some time examining the place they'd shaved bare but did no more than stir up a little longing for the warrior's earlier return. Wrapping myself in a pelt, I sat and stayed warm by the fire. I found myself staring at the flames in a trance—but without a dreadful vision. With Dagg and Svein around, I was safe.

Things were going better than I dared hope, but there were still challenges. The time would come when my mates would mark me, and then what? Winter would not last forever. We belonged back on the mountain, with the pack. I missed my friends, and surely Dagg and Svein would wish to be accepted by their fellow warriors.

An earthy grunt caught my ears, and I wandered to the front of the cave. Booted footprints led away, but there was no sign of the warriors. Only a slight rustle in the forest beyond. I pulled a pelt around me and ventured out.

There, hunched behind a few holly bushes. Was that black fur?

"Dagg?"

Had he returned? Was he no longer a man, but a monster?

The creature ambled out from behind the bracken and I froze. It wasn't a Berserker monster, but a bear, woken before it's time. Lean, angry, and very, very hungry.

Slowly, I took a step back. There was a chance it would not see or scent me, or that it would smell the fire on me and stay away.

A half step back, and another. The animal grunted and shuffled closer. It had found something interesting under the bush. The bones from a past meal. Dagg had left them there. As I stood there, willing myself to inch further toward the cave, the bear lumbered along the edge of the bushes, sniffing for more bones, and suddenly was between me and the cave. It went on ripping and gnawing at its newfound meal, while my eyes darted around, frantically looking for an escape route.

The bear shuffled around the front of the cave, grunting at the fire smell. Then it's head swung to me.

I ran before it charged. Branches whipped my face as I crashed into the bracken, the bear a dark shape behind. I fought free of the briars holding me and raced into the forest, zig zagging between the pines.

A grunt behind me. The bear was gaining ground. It was big and hungry, and I was lost on unfamiliar terrain. Snow sucked at my boots, dragging me down, and I staggered, wrenching my body forward as fast as I could.

Dark fur flashed to my right and I veered away, only to collide with something white and solid and warm. Not a snow drift. It lifted me while my legs still pumped and held me fast. I screamed, clawing and fighting, but it held me easily, clutching me to its great body.

Be still. Golden eyes pinned me. The creature holding me was big with white and grey fur. It had a wolf's muzzle and shaggy body rising up on two legs, taller than any man.

A growl shook the air and went through me. Two dark forms rose up and clashed together. The bear and... something else. Another monster covered in dark fur.

"Dagg," I breathed as the dark monster roared loud enough to shake snow from the trees. The bear turned and ran. Dagg dropped to all fours, shrinking a little into the form of a wolf.

The white and grey monster huffed and started striding back to the cave.

"Svein," I murmured as he cradled me in his arms. I traced the monstrous features, the fur lined neck, the sleek muzzle. Golden eyes watched me explore. When I got close to his teeth, canines long as knives, he turned his head and nipped at my fingers. By the time we returned, his form was a man's, not as big but just as powerful. The Change left a white and grey fur across his shoulders. As soon as we entered the cave, he tossed the pelt down.

"What—" I started to ask, when he whirled and advanced, looming over me. He put his hands on my neckline and tore my gown straight down the front. Too shocked to speak, I stood shivering in my shift as he pawed over me, the animal qualities of his face receding further.

A dark hulking form entered the cave. Dagg. His hands were more bear like than human and tipped with scythe like claws.

I heard clearly their voices in my mind.

She must be punished. They agreed and turned their golden gaze on me.

I swallowed and stepped back. *Dagg and Svein,* I reminded myself. *Dagg and Svein.* They would not hurt me.

Are you so sure, little red? Svein's growl held amusement. Again, I had the impression he'd spoken but heard not words.

You broke your word. You left the cave. Svein's face bore no trace of humor.

"I only—"

Take off your shift. Now, he added when I hesitated.

I stripped in haste, lest he tear it again as easy as breaking a cobweb.

Now go to the pelts, all fours. Arse in the air.

I dropped to the bed and scrambled to obey. My neck prickled at the incredibly vulnerable position. On all fours with a cheek pressed to the pelts, my haunches were exposed. They could do anything they liked with me.

As I thought this, a large hand rested on my bottom. Fingers lightly bit in to my flesh and drew downwards. If he was in beast form, the claws would leave bloody furrows. How easy it would be for the monsters to deliver death.

Oh, little red, we will not harm you, not in that way. But there are consequences. The hands settled on my hips and propped them higher. Hot breath gusted over my lower lips.

Teeth, the canines long and not quite human, nibbled on my exposed center.

A large body laid out beside me. I kept my head down in case looking around would not please them. The mouth between my legs kept up its leisurely exploration. A large finger brushed my breast. My breath caught as a claw traced a lazy circle around my nipple. I was shivering for a different reason than cold. In fact, in the past few minutes, it'd grown very warm.

"You do well to obey us," Dagg murmured at my side.

"I didn't mean to run into danger."

"You've been running into danger since the night you came to us," Svein sounded stern. "And we are grateful. But it ends now."

"You want us to protect you. We will."

Dagg kept fondling my breasts as Svein's fingers skimmed the line of my buttocks. Ripples of sensation shot straight through my core.

"Relax. I'm going to punish you now."

Svein set my knees a few inches wider, giving him ample access to me. "This is ours," he murmured, sliding up the inside of my legs to cup my pulsing core. "And this."

"Yes," I whispered.

Slowly, he slid a finger in. My muscles tightened around the intruder. After running the single digit around the edge of my needy opening, he added another. And another. The fourth pressed in soon after, stretching me.

"Ohhh," I whimpered at the invasion, just on the edge of discomfort

"Calm," Dagg stroked down my spine until I relaxed.

"That's it." Svein now had his fingers tight together, fitting all of them into the tight entrance to my body. "Open, little red. Open to me.

He pressed in and the uncomfortable stretch turned into an overwhelming sensation. I whimpered as my body flexed around him, little muscles tightening with pleasure.

Slowly, Svein retreated, murmuring something I didn't hear.

"Let me," Dagg murmured and the shadows moved over me as they switched places.

Hot breath hit my nethers, strong fingers holding my legs apart when I would squirm. Instead of fingers, his tongue worked in the furrows around my sex, finding the secret spots that pulled soft moans from my mouth as pleasure burned through me.

Large hands lifted and positioned me, gentle as if handling a bird's egg. They set me on my back, then rose up on either side of me, mountains of shadow with golden eyes.

Svein set his hand at my entrance again. His fingers were slick and this time, he easily pushed inside.

"Deep breath," he ordered, and with it, pushed inside me. I shook. Rivulets of pleasure ran from deep inside me, spreading through my whole body.

"Too much?" Svein asked. He was inside me, his hand filling me. My entranced stretched around his wrist.

I wanted to thrash and cry because it wasn't too much, it wasn't enough. I was full, every part of me, and I only wanted more. I wanted these men to fill me up, mind body and soul. I wanted to drown.

Pleasure burned through my mind. It seized and shook me so hard my back spasmed. Svein's fist touched every part of me.

I was floating in another world when he withdrew. The warrior's chuckles wafted above me.

Dagg propped me up and gave me water, his beard tickling my bare chest. I tugged him to me, nuzzling blindly at his face until I found his lips.

"You did well," he murmured. "Will you mind from now on?"

My head rolled against his forehead as I nodded.

"Good girl."

He rose up and I blinked in to the dark. The two warriors loomed over me, pulling at their cocks, their eyes fixed on me. One by one, they spent, splashing on my bare skin.

"Rub it in, little one. Take our scent. Everyone will know who you belong to."

Dagg lay down beside me, turning me so my body fit against his. His coarse hair rubbed against my skin, sending prickles of awareness through my sated body.

"Sleep in peace, little dove. You're ours, now."

I sank into sleep, his voice echoing into my dreams. *We own you.*

I STOOD ON A CLIFF, *staring down at the world far below. My skirts whipped in the wind that shrieked along the heights. Below, the Corpse King's army fought the Berserkers. Sword beat shield, axe cleaved bone. The wind carried the sound of battle and the stench of the undead.*

"It's over," the Corpse King said. He stood at my back, black robes swathing his bony self. His mirage was slipping—he looked more like the undead he commanded than the human mage he'd once been. "You may as well give it to me."

My hand closed over the jewel at my neck. Eldritch light escaped from between my fingers.

"It does not belong to him." There was a third on the cliff, a

woman with white gold hair. "Give it to your sisters, so we may *all defeat him.*"

I opened my hand, and the stone had disappeared. I still saw it clearly, shimmering at the bottom of a pool.

I opened my mouth to tell the woman.

"No," the mage king screamed, and threw a cloud of shadow at me. "Don't speak."

I felt a hand wrap about my mouth, choking my breath. I could not even scream—

I was halfway up and across the cave before the warriors found their feet.

"What is it, little dove?"

I shook my head, my head pounding with the Corpse King's command. *Don't speak. Don't speak.* Horrible things would come to pass if I let loose my voice.

Squinting through the pain in my temples, I stooped and drew on my boots.

"Where are you going?"

I grabbed my cup and little pot and tossed it into the sack but got no further. Dagg caught me fast.

"You're not going anywhere," he growled.

Svein frowned. "You are upset. Will you tell us why?"

I shook my head. Tremors went through me. How had the Corpse King found me? My mates were supposed to keep the dreams at bay.

"Please," Svein squatted before me. "Tell us what you fear. We would share this burden with you."

I pressed my hands over my mouth. I felt the mage's spell again, covering my mouth so my own screams filled my throat and choked me.

"Something's wrong," Dagg said gruffly. A low growl started rumbling in his chest.

"Fern," Svein said. "if you tell us we can help you. Did something startle you?"

Dagg rose abruptly and started pacing, pausing only to raise his head. "Do you smell that?"

Was that a whiff of rot? Were the visions so bad they conjured the mage? Was he here?

This was my final fear: that the dreams would turn real.

I shivered hard and Svein tucked a pelt around me

"Was it a dream? Like the one you had before, when we were on the run from the abbey?"

"You were supposed to stop them," I blurted, panting with the pain in my chest. "You were supposed to keep me safe."

"We have failed you again, little one." He pulled me into his arms, and I struggled.

"No, I must go. The visions will continue to come, until they are real." it was my fault. I drew the dreams, and they grew more solid until they'd come to pass. Time and time again, it had happened. I'd seen the destruction of the abbey, the kidnapping of my friends. The Corpse King coming for the Berserkers in the mist. Then it had all happened, and I'd been powerless to stop it.

I had to go. I was a danger to everyone I cared about.

"Let us fight for you. Let us keep you safe."

"No," I wept. "I cannot. He will come for me and I will never be safe."

"Who?

"The Corpse King," Dagg growled. He stopped pacing, his limbs going stiff. With a great groan, he threw his head back. His face reshaped, bones popping with the Change.

"Dagg," Svein barked. "Not here—run!"

The dark-furred monster rushed outside and roared.

27

F ern

I SAT BY THE FIRE, my heart sick. Svein had gone out for a time, to find Dagg after his rampage. He made me promise to stay put and took my boots for good measure. I didn't move. I was too tired and wrung out to run.

The visions had found me, even here. My mates did nothing to stop them. They would continue to get worse. Then the fits would come. Better for me to beg to be put down. I knew how Dagg felt, at the mercy of the battle rage.

Footsteps came to the cave, along with the scent of pine and fur. The warriors returning, stomping to make sure I heard them. Two pairs of boots came to my side, but I still didn't look up. Dagg must be all right, if he'd returned. If I was lucky, he wouldn't hate me for bringing on the madness.

They should send me away. The next time the visions came, the madness might take Dagg forever. It would've been better had I been burned as a witch by the nuns, then bring this evil to ones I loved. They could've chosen another spaewife for themselves. The pain that thought brought nearly crippled me.

Svein set my boots down near me. "We have decided. You will tell us the visions you see."

My shoulders slumped. *Don't speak, don't speak.* My head hurt with a piercing pain.

"Fern," Gentle hands settled on my head, eclipsing the ache. "You will obey."

What did it matter, if I was to die?

"I see the Corpse King, only he is made of mist and bones. There are often women—ghosts—who try to guide me. I have a jewel on a chain I must keep safe."

"Good girl," Svein murmured, and the stabbing in my head lessened.

"The Corpse King wants the jewel. I don't know why, only that he wants it. No one has it though," I tried to remember the last of my dream. "It is lost. Hidden some-where." The image came to me again. "At the bottom of a pool."

There was a long silence. I waited for the warriors to denounce me and take my head. Or perhaps they'd just throw me out to die. It would not take more than a few hours in this cold. It'd be quick.

"What is this stone?" Svein mused, almost to himself.

"It's white, with a little blue. Sometimes it glows," I said.

Dagg growled, until Svein nudged him. Then the sound cut off.

"The pack must know of this," Svein said. "Soon. We must send a message."

"But then they will find you," I quavered.

"Perhaps. Perhaps not. Maybe they'll see how our mate returned us to sanity. How you saved us."

"I have not saved you. I have brought evil into your midst."

"Enough. It is not your fault. We know how to drive the Corpse King away."

I lifted my head. "How?"

"We will mark you. Claim you forever as ours."

Dagg knelt. His eyes were bright, his beard unruly, but he was every inch a man. Rough fingers brushed at my cheeks, dashing away my tears. "You belong to us."

I shook my head sadly.

"Once you begged for our mark."

Before. Now I could not stand the thought of sharing my nightmares with them. They should cast me out as my family had.

I covered my face and wept.

"Enough," Dagg said and tugged me to his lap. He held me a long time, rubbing my back, soothing me. Svein brought me a cup of tea, and then a plate of stew. Dagg fed me.

As I ate, the two conversed without speaking. This was the brother bond I'd so hoped would return. The fact that I could hear it meant our mating bond was almost complete. All that was missing was the mating mark.

We must claim her. If the Corpse King wages war in her mind, we must defend her. Both of us. If I fall—

I will not let you, brother. If we fall, we fall together. Together we will be stronger, Svein vowed.

Perhaps the Alphas will help us.

And if they do not? What if the pack comes for her?

Dagg bared his teeth. *We will fight.*

After dinner, Svein washed my face and hands, then cupped my cheek and studied me for a long time.

"You belong to us," he murmured. "We won't let you go."

I roused a little. "It's too late," I said tiredly. "Let me leave. He will come and find me, and I will lead him to you, and the others. That's what he wants. He needs a bride to fuel his power." As I spoke the words, I realized they were true. My instincts to run from the mountain, the heart of the Berserker territory, would save my friends. I would not be the weakness that allowed the Corpse King access to them.

Svein lifted the hair from my neck and cradled the base of my skull. One twist and he'd snap my neck. I closed my eyes. I should beg him to do it.

"No. You are safe here. We will defend you with our lives."

"You belong to us, little dove," Dagg murmured at my back. His large hands skimmed down my legs, outlining them under my gown. "Your body is ours." Even in my despair, my body responded, quickening. "It knows its masters."

Svein started to lift me and I struggled. It was like a leaf fighting a gale.

"Do not hurt yourself," the warriors crooned as they stripped me bare and laid me down. Dagg lay down behind me and pulled me against his body, surrounding me with his strength. For a while we lay like that, his warmth infusing me. He played with my hair, stroking it from the back of my neck until I was attuned to his touch.

Hot breath blew over the vulnerable spot at the base of my neck. "Tonight we show you how much we own your body."

I let out a sigh. Excitement buzzed through me despite myself.

His fingers strayed to my front, finding my breasts and rolling the nipples one by one. "You brought us back to ourselves. Now we will claim you. The circle will be complete."

A few nuzzling kisses at my nape and I was so relaxed I barely protested when Dagg rose and Svein arranged me on my back.

"I trust you will not move from where I place you."

I shook my head languidly.

"If you do I will tie you down."

A quiver went through me. Svein bent and kissed me, trailing kisses down my body. He settled between my legs, nibbling the inside of one thigh, then the other, holding me down when I jerked. He licked me teasingly and then flipped me over, kissing down my sensitive spine. My bottom rocked against him, pushing up against his hard cock. He grasped my hips to keep me still, trailing his tongue down past the apex of my buttocks to dip into the cleft.

"What?" I gasped and wriggled to get away.

A hard hand cracked against my bottom. Svein pulled back and took his time dispensing correction, spanking my bare cheeks until the stinging heat made me drip shamefully.

"Will you submit to me?"

"Yes," I cried.

He explored between my legs. "Wet," he announced with satisfaction.

"Barely a punishment," Dagg chuckled.

"So sweet. Your body knows who owns it." Svein parted my bottom cheeks and licked between them.

"Oh no," I moaned as his tongue circled my lower hole. It was shameful, how good it felt.

"You love it. You're soaking," he said in wonder. His other hand stroked over my wet lower lips as his mouth plundered my naughty back hole. He paused to nibble on my left buttock. "I like your cheeks red. When you disobey I'll take pleasure correcting you."

"She takes pleasure, too," Dagg murmured. His hands brushed my swaying breasts, just enough touch to make me want more.

"Please," I breathed.

"What is it you want, little red?" Svein asked, wicked humor in his voice.

I lifted my bottom. Flushed hot as I begged silently for them to take me.

"And if I decide I wish to claim you here?" He probed my back hole with a thick finger. I pressed my face into the pelts and moaned.

"So sweet and obedient. I'll make you come with my mouth on your cunny and my fingers in your bottom hole."

"Ohhh..."

"Beg me."

"Please make me cum..."

He laid a light slap on my throbbing cheek. "How?"

"With your mouth... on my cunny."

"And?"

"Your fingers in my bottom," I whispered, cheeks aflame.

"Good girl. Roll over. I'll give you what you need."

I was spared the sight of Svein's wicked mouth and fingers stroking me by Dagg, who bent and claimed my mouth. He waited until I gasped my pleasure to present his cock to my lips.

"Your turn to please us," he murmured and came into me slowly as I moaned. Svein kept fondling me as I sucked Dagg's cock. I clenched around his fingers.

"Greedy," Svein murmured, and took his hand away. A second later, he set his cock at my wet entrance. "I'll give you what you need."

For all their size, the two warriors were gentle. Dagg kept light fingers on my face, guiding me to lick him as he pleased. I would've blushed to serve him this way, but with Svein thrusting the promise of pleasure hovering just out of reach, I was eager to please.

All too soon, Dagg withdrew from my mouth, his rod hard and stiff.

"What—" I started to ask, when they propped me up between them. Svein settled me firmly on him, filling me even more. Dagg pressed against my back, playing with my hair.

"The mating bite," he breathed at my nape. Prickles went up and down my neck.

"I am not—"

Svein rolled his hips under me, sending his cock surging deeper, and I lost the ability to speak.

Twin canines pressed against my vulnerable shoulder. Svein rose up and smoothed my hair away from the other side. His hips kept rocking, making me ride him to completion as the two held me fast with firm hands, and bit down.

A second of pain, an instant of hovering on the precipice. My breath whistled between my teeth, body clenching. It was too much for Svein, who came, bucking wildly

He bent me forward and Dagg worked his cock at my back, grunting as his seed splashed me. He spread it around, dipping between my buttocks to tease my back hole.

"One day soon we will take you here," he promised.

I lay limp on Svein, panting. The marks on my shoulders

sizzled and burned, but the skin had already healed. Four slight red weals were the only sign I'd been marked.

It'll be enough to warn any Berserker away from you. And the Corpse King, should he trespass where he doesn't belong.

I blinked at Dagg, realizing he'd heard my thoughts.

That's right, little dove. We're joined now. Svein and I will make sure nothing keeps us apart.

I'd never be alone again. Never wake from a bad dream and have no one to comfort me. My mates would bear the burden along with me. There was no way to stop it. There was nothing I could do but to wait for a vision to come.

28

D^{agg}

A MAN who escapes death takes no moment for granted. When I woke beside my mate, her red hair spilled across my chest, I did not hurry to rise. The fire needed tending, Svein and I needed to hunt, but it wouldn't do to risk waking Fern. She slept as if wrung out from fighting a great battle. Which, in a way, we had. I stroked her soft hair and savored the moment. After all, it was the least I could do to let her rest.

Besides, my cock was so hard, the slightest brush against her legs while rising would have me spilling like an untried youth.

On the other side of our mate, Svein chuckled. *Go ahead, Dagg. When she wakes, I'll be the one to pleasure her. I'm man enough to wait.*

Grabbing a pelt, I flung it hard enough to whip Svein in the face while missing Fern. He laughed louder.

Quiet, you lump. You're as loud as a boar crashing in brush.

What am I then? Svein taunted. *A lump or a boar?*

You're useless as a handless axe.

Those can be quite useful. I remember this one battle—

Between us our mate jerked in her sleep. The two of us were on instant alert, but after a moment she quieted. She settled against me again, her breathing going soft once more.

The Alphas need to know what she is. We need to tell them.

I know. I threaded red strands between my fingers. *She's a volva, a seeress.*

I'm surprised we didn't guess when she first had the dream. Remember, in the mists?

She must tell the pack of her visions. They may hold a clue to defeating the Corpse King. She may save us.

Not us. If we returned to the mountain, our fellow Berserkers may kill us, and take our mate from us.

The beast inside me said we must fight to prevent it. But with the whole pack against us, we would fail.

She cannot stay here. She is not meant to live in a cave.

I cursed to myself, but Svein was right.

We will return her to the pack. Today. The pelt slipped from one white shoulder and I covered her again, though it pained me to do it. In summer I would refuse to allow her to dress. I'd make her lay naked within the line of my sight, just so I could have beauty to look upon in every moment.

If I lived to summer.

When she wakes, we will bundle her up and carry her to the nearest scouting post. Perhaps we have a few friends among the pack who will vouch for us.

A twig snapped outside. The few winter birds sheltered in the bushes nearby flew away. Someone was approaching the cave.

"Or they will come to us," Svein said, and cursed.

"See to our mate," I rose as a Berserker called for me.

"Dagg the Black. Come out and show yourself."

I rose, deliberately leaving my axe.

"Come out if you have honor."

"I have honor," I called and stepped out of the cave.

An arrow flew and lodged itself in my right shoulder. I grunted. It burned but hadn't hit anything vital. Not that it mattered. My Berserker healing was back, returned to me by my mate.

As I pulled the arrow from my flesh, the leader, a strong warrior named Knut, turned and grabbed the bow from the attacking warrior. "You fool, why'd you shoot him? He isn't a threat."

"It's all right," I said, showing them I could be calm. "I don't blame Grimr for being afraid of me. Besides, he's a poor shot."

The ensembled warriors chuckled, some of them nervously.

"So, Dagg." Knut fixed me with a hard look. "You are well."

"Well enough."

"We are here because you are camped too close to the mountain. The Alphas wish you to move."

I shrugged. "I am happy to go. Svein will come. It is only..." Gasps told me Svein had emerged, carrying Fern. "Our mate is very sensitive to the cold. And she wishes to be close to her friends. You understand."

"You will hand the woman over," Knut's tone had changed. Become more dangerous.

"No," Fern said softly. "I won't go. Tell them, Svein."

"She is our mate," I declared.

"Lies," the man who'd shot me called out. Grimr. He had

not gotten a woman in the raid, and he coveted mine. I ignored him, and so did the rest of the warriors.

"This is not the place to keep a mate," Knut said. He would try to carry out his orders and do the right thing. A good man, and a good warrior.

"I agree. We were upset when we learned she had come down the mountain to find us."

"She came to us in a blizzard, Knut," Svein added. "We had hoped the pack would take better care of her."

A warrior, tall and lean with a tanned face, stepped out. "She was well cared for. She snuck out in the blizzard and her friends kept her absence a secret. Fern, come to me. Your friends are worried about you."

"I won't go," she said, clutching Svein's shoulders. "I am where I belong."

Knut sighed. "I do not wish to spill blood."

"I do not wish to fight, either. Our mate is delicate. She does not belong around violence."

"But you will not give her up."

Svein and I exchanged glances. We had a decision to make. One that might mean our death.

But Fern's life was more important.

"Take us to the Alphas," I said. "Let them pass judgement."

29

D^{agg}

WE WERE HALFWAY up the mountain when it happened. A choking sound rose up. I whirled and found three spears pointed at my chest. They let Svein carry Fern, but we were surrounded.

"What is happening?" I bellowed to him.

Our mate lay limp in Svein's arms. Her eyes rolled back, showing only whites under her lids. Her entire body convulsed.

We could only watch helpless as the vision took her.

Svein cradled Fern to him.

"Get them away from her. They're hurting her."

"Stop," the warrior Jarl cried. He pushed through our guard to get close. "One of the spaewives says she often falls into trances. It happened before we raided the abbey."

"What sort of fit is this?" Knut growled. I tried to step between him and our mate, sensing the threat in his voice. Simple warriors would distrust anything strange. Natural wolves would put a rabid one down.

Weapons swung toward me before I took two steps.

"It is not a fit," Svein said. "Do not touch her."

"Quickly," I barked, frozen with my hands out to show I meant no harm. "We must get her to a witch."

"Up the mountain," the warriors ordered. I growled in frustration and the spears pricked my skin.

"There is a witch there. One of the Alphas mates," Knut said quickly.

"How do we know they haven't done this to her?" Grimr muttered but as we sped up the path, he fell behind. Knut's friends, Leif, Rolf, and Thorbjorn, clustered around Svein.

I followed, gritting my teeth. My mate was in the throes of a vision, and I could not help her. The wind blew by, carrying the stench of corpses. Damn, but I did not like the mage's hold on my mate.

We burst into the clearing, where the Alphas already assembled. Samuel sat on his throne, his mate sitting on a smaller rock beside him, holding his hand. The rest of the leaders stood beside them. Judge, jury, and executioners, all arrayed.

Svein came to the center of the circle and crouched with Fern still in his arms. I pushed to their side, helping him arrange her, supporting her head until someone said, "Enough."

I growled, and an axe came to my throat. Just then Fern opened her eyes.

"Dagg," she whispered.

"It's all right," I told her gruffly. "We are here on the

mountain. You had a vision. The Alphas will ask you what you Saw."

Her face went white.

"You do not have to tell them anything," I spoke carefully around the axe edge at my throat. "But if you do, they will not hurt you, I swear it."

30

F ern

My worst nightmare had come true. I'd fallen into a trance and woke up in the middle of a crowd. No one spoke, and everyone seemed to be watching me.

The Alphas were there, and all the warriors, death written on their faces. If someone gave the kill order, Dagg and Svein would not survive.

I had to speak. I had no choice.

"I will speak," I said, and on the ledge beside the rocky mountain face, my voice carried.

Under the pelt I wore as a cloak, I found Svein's hand and gripped it. His face betrayed no tension, but he held tight.

"I am Fern, a spaewife. I have... dreams." Someone slipped to the lead Alpha's side, leaned in and whispered. Perhaps explaining who I was, or perhaps giving an argument for my mate's death. I had to say something that might sway the pack to my mate's side.

"The Corpse King comes to me at night. In my dreams. I have met him there for some time. Ever since I left the abbey."

Murmurs went around the pack, and one of the Alphas barked for silence.

That's it, little dove. Tell them everything. We will keep you safe.

"There was a time when the dreams were under control —the days I was with Dagg and Svein. But then the Corpse King attacked them, and drove them mad, and they were banished."

"They attacked a group of us," a warrior spoke up. "Vik and I were there."

On his throne, the lead Alpha waved his hand for silence.

"When I was separated from my mates," I raised my voice. "My dreams returned. They plagued me during the day." I sought Jarl's face in the crowd. "Ask my friends... they will tell you what they saw. The only way for the visions to stop was to return to my mates. So I left and found them."

A deep growl thundered from one of the warriors who'd come for Dagg. "You climbed down the mountain, alone?"

I wouldn't have the courage to answer him if Svein had not been near.

"Yes." I turned to Jarl. "I found my way down slowly. I snuck out when the guards were busy with the snow. They would not notice me. It's not their fault."

The Alpha on the throne planted his elbows on his thighs and leaned forward. Everyone held their breath, waiting for him to speak. All except the brown-haired woman who sat beside him. His mate put her hand on his leg. One touch and the Alpha seemed to think better of what he would say. "Speak on," he commanded. His tone wasn't unkind.

"I found Svein... and together we convinced Dagg to stay with us." I smiled, remembering those few days when the hardest battle was the snow and cold and wolf who would not come near the fire. "My mates grew strong. Their beast was under control. They never hurt me."

Someone was muttering, "She doesn't know her own mind."

Growls broke out around me. I clutched at Svein.

Calm yourself, little red. They are angry on your behalf. The Alphas bade you speak and none should interrupt.

The men around Dagg had lowered their weapons. He nodded to me, encouraging. I stood up, keeping a hand on Svein's shoulder to steady me.

"Listen to what I have to say," I shouted, and the ensemble went dead silent. They would listen, and they would decide whether to kill us.

"I had another vision, even by my mate's side. And again, while I was coming up the mountain." The wind rose as I spoke, and goosebumps rose on my arms. I shouted louder. "The Corpse King is waiting to attack. He gathers his strength. He tests our defenses, looking for weakness. I was weak because I did not trust my own mind. I needed the protection of my mates. But together, we will stand strong."

I looked dead in the eye of the lead Alpha. "The mage seeks a stone, this big," I showed him my fist. "And milky white. It glows sometimes. I Saw it lying at the bottom of a deep pool. The mage will use it... somehow." I slumped a little, the energy leaving me. I did not have all the answers they would seek, but I had done my part.

The wind had risen, tearing at my face. Ice like needles

fell from the sky. The Berserkers raised their shields against the sleet.

A cry rang out. A woman stood, arms outstretched over the assembly, chanting loudly. The wind whipped her honey blonde hair and skirts. Two Alphas stood behind her, hands out to support her.

The storm left as quickly as it'd blown up. On the throne, the Alpha had wet hair and cuts on his face from the ice that were already healing. He checked on his mate, who'd crouched with a second Alpha. They all straightened, faces calm and unshaken.

"She speaks of the moonstone," the blonde woman said. She'd stopped the wind, so she was something of a witch. She'd be Sabine, one of the first Berserker mates. A spaewife with great powers. "The witches have all gathered to find what might defeat the mage. The moonstone is our only hope, but we must find it. Now we know it can be found, and that it lies at the bottom of a pool." She looked straight at me. "Thank you, Fern." With that, she wobbled a little on her feet, and her two mates came to support her. One, a burly man covered with bluish tattoos, swung her into his arms and strode into the cave.

"The moonstone," the lead Alpha mused.

"I have heard only a spaewife can find it." A silver-haired warrior said. "Perhaps this is her."

"Our mate sees visions only. She is not the one to leave the mountain, but perhaps, in time, she will know more clues."

"Truly, she has a gift from the goddess. She is not mad," The one-eyed warrior said. "She has a gift."

"Enough," the lead Alpha said. "I have heard enough." He stood, and his mate stood with him. Her eyes on mine were kind.

I waited, trembling for what judgement would fall.

"Fern of the Berserkers," he said. "You have a sacred place in this pack as a seer, and our protection. Any wolf will defend you to the death, for someday, your visions may save all our lives. Thank you for speaking. You honor us," he added, in a quieter tone, as if it was meant only for me.

Tears pricked my eyes.

"Dagg and Svein. Stand for your judgement."

My mates stood. I reached for their hands. Whatever judgement fell we would face it together. If they were banished, I would leave with them. If they tried to keep me from them, I would escape. I would find a way. My destiny was twofold: to be a seer, and their mate. I would not stay with a pack that kept me from them.

It's all right, Fern. Dagg squeezed my hand.

"You fought long and hard for this pack. Another fight is coming—the greatest battle we have known. But you have a special role." He pointed at me. "The goddess has blessed us with a seer. A treasure, indeed. You are to be her guardians. Keep her safe, above all."

"Above our lives, Alpha. So we pledge." Striking their fists to their hearts, they turned and carried me away. I grabbed at their shoulders to steady myself, surprise and relief running through me.

The warriors around us shouted—some with glee, some angry. Some called for an attack on the Corpse King, some on my mates. The Alphas were on their feet, trying to restore order.

Dagg and Svein kept walking. A few of the warriors who'd brought us here closed around us, offering protection.

"This way," one waved us at a fork on the mountain path. The group broke into a run and I clung tight to Dagg.

"Where are you taking me?"

"You'll see,"

"What about the cave? Our things..."

"We'll send someone to get them. Do you wish to stay there, or in the lodge we built for you?"

I jerked in Dagg's arm. "What?"

"Did we not tell you we would bring our mate to a lodge? We built it before we came to find you."

Stunned, I held on as the warriors veered off the path, kicking through the drifts. They seemed lighthearted, chatting and calling each other as they forged a new route through the snow. It seemed my journey had come full circle, once again being carried to my new home, safe in my mate's arms.

"There," Svein pointed up to a ledge where a log building rose from the snow, smoke drifting from a hole in the roof.

"As soon as the Alphas passed judgement, we sent word to make ready," one of the warriors explained to us.

"It'll be quite a climb," observed another. "Why did you build it on such a high ledge?"

"Privacy," Svein said with a grin that made my cheeks heat.

The warriors fell silent then, focused on the climb. I noted landmarks—a twisted tree here, a great boulder there, as we wound up the mountain to the home my mates had built.

The lodge was built with a sharply sloped roof, jutting out from the side of the mountain. A fresh trail broke through the snow to the doorstep and as we grew close a dark-haired woman stepped out to greet us.

"Fern!" Laurel called. She stood swathed in a long cloak,

her cheeks rosy above the fur collar. Her two mates followed, greeting their warrior friends.

Dagg let me down just as Laurel rushed up and threw her arms around me.

"I'm so glad you've returned. We were so worried." She drew back. "Let me look at you. You are well?"

"I am."

She hugged me again. "I'm glad. We left bread for you," she whispered in my ear. "My mates smelled the crumbs and realized what you were doing. They approved."

"Thank you," I whispered back. She had left the bread and the honey.

"You must be exhausted. We'll leave you now. I just wanted to leave you a welcome gift."

She drew me inside the dark lodge. The place smelled of new wood and smoke. Someone had started a fire in the stone firepit. Warriors streamed in and out, carrying wood stacking it close by.

"Here," Laurel pointed out two baskets covered in cloth. "Sweet bread and meat pies. That should be enough until your mates are ready to hunt again."

"Thank you," I choked out past a lump in my throat.

Laurel hugged me again and left with her mates, holding their hands as they helped her through the snow.

"The Alphas will want to speak to our seer again," the warrior Knut said to my mates. "The witches, too. They want to find the moonstone, so we are prepared for the Corpse King's coming attack. We have until spring."

"Later," Dagg said. "Once our mate is rested."

With final grins and slaps on the back, Knut and the rest of the warriors marched away.

"Well, Fern?" Svein stood in the center of the lodge, one boot resting on the stone ring around the fire pit. Smoke drifted up and out of a hole in the roof. "What do you think of your new home?"

I nodded, tears pricking my eyes. Tears of happiness.

"Lost her voice again," Svein commented.

"It's all right," Dagg said gruffly. I knew he felt as overwhelmed as I did. "We will help her find it again."

There was a bed in the back of the lodge, already heaped with pelts. Dagg propped me on it and cupped my head in his great hands.

"You did it. You spoke loud and clear."

Swallowing hard, I nodded.

"And you will do it again. We will stand by you when the Alphas call you to consult."

"Our mate, seeress for the pack," Dagg spoke with great pride. He kissed my forehead, his beard tickling me.

"Were you frightened?"

"Yes," I tried to remember. Once I'd opened my mouth, the words had flown out. "But after I spoke, I was not afraid."

"We will call the witch Yseult. She will come and teach you how to use your gift. She will help you find your voice."

"I've already found it." And I had.

My mates had given it back to me.

~

Thank you for reading this book! I have several more Berserker bride books to write, including books for Sorrel, Juliet and Rosalind! Read on for an excerpt from Tamed by the Berserkers. Much love to the Berserker fans who motivate me to continue the series. I appreciate you.

Smooches,

Lee

FREE BOOK

Get two secret Berserker books, Bred by the Berserkers and
A Berserker Birth, available exclusively to you:

https://geni.us/BredBerserkerNONL
https://geni.us/BirthBerserkerNONL

A NOTE FROM LEE SAVINO

Hey there. It's me, Lee Savino. I'm so glad you read this book and ordered it directly from my store. Readers like you make my author life possible! And being an author is a dream come true.

If you're like me, you're wondering what to read next. Let me help you out...

If you haven't yet, check out the two exclusive extras I wrote in the Berserker world. They're available here:

Bred by the Berserkers
https://geni.us/BredBerserkerNONL

A Berserker Birth
https://geni.us/BirthBerserkerNONL

And if you want more Berserkers, you can find the complete selection at my store or get the 15 book bundle here!

WANT MORE BERSERKERS?

These fierce warriors will stop at nothing to claim their mates...

Get a 15 e-book Berserker bundle on sale at my Lee Savino shop!

The Berserker Saga

Sold to the Berserkers – Brenna, Samuel & Daegan
Mated to the Berserkers – Brenna, Samuel & Daegan
Bred by the Berserkers (FREE novella only available to you)
– Brenna, Samuel & Daegan
Taken by the Berserkers – Sabine, Ragnvald & Maddox
Given to the Berserkers – Muriel and her mates
Claimed by the Berserkers – Fleur and her mates
Rescued by the Berserker – Hazel & Knut
Captured by the Berserkers – Willow, Leif & Brokk
Kidnapped by the Berserkers – Sage, Thorbjorn & Rolf
Bonded to the Berserkers – Laurel, Haakon & Ulf

Berserker Babies – the sisters Brenna, Sabine, Muriel, Fleur
and their mates
Night of the Berserkers – the witch Yseult's story
Owned by the Berserkers – Fern, Dagg & Svein
Tamed by the Berserkers – Sorrel, Thorsteinn & Vik
Mastered by the Berserkers – Juliet, Jarl & Fenrir
Surrendered to the Berserkers – Rosalind and her mates

Berserker Warriors

Ægir *(formerly titled The Sea Wolf)*
Siebold with Ines Johnson

ALSO BY LEE SAVINO

For film and TV rights inquiries: lee.savino@leesavino.com

$\sim$

Paranormal romance

Berserker Saga

Sold to the Berserkers

Mated to the Berserkers

Bred by the Berserkers (FREE novella only available at
www.leesavino.com)

Taken by the Berserkers

Given to the Berserkers

Claimed by the Berserkers

Rescued by the Berserker

Captured by the Berserkers

Kidnapped by the Berserkers

Bonded to the Berserkers

Berserker Babies

Night of the Berserkers

Owned by the Berserkers

Tamed by the Berserkers

Mastered by the Berserkers

Surrendered to the Berserkers

Berserker Warriors

Aegir

Siebold with Ines Johnson

Bad Boy Alphas with Renee Rose

Alpha's Temptation

Alpha's Danger

Alpha's Prize

Alpha's Challenge

Alpha's Obsession

Alpha's Desire

Alpha's War

Alpha's Mission

Alpha's Bane

Alpha's Secret

Alpha's Prey

Alpha's Sun

Shifter Ops with Renee Rose

Alpha's Moon

Alpha's Vow

Alpha's Revenge

Alpha's Fire

Alpha's Rescue

Alpha's Command

Midnight Doms with Renee Rose

Alpha's Blood

His Captive Mortal

The Virgin and the Vampire

(All Souls' Night anthology exclusive)

Werewolves of Wallstreet with Renee Rose

Big Bad Boss: Midnight

Big Bad Boss: Moon Mad

Big Bad Boss: Marked

~

Sci fi romance

Planet of Kings with Tabitha Black

Brutal Mate

Brutal Claim

Brutal Capture

Brutal Beast

Brutal Demon

Tsenturion Warriors with Golden Angel

Alien Captive

Alien Tribute

Alien Abduction

Dragons in Exile with Lili Zander

Draekon Mate

Draekon Fire

Draekon Heart

Draekon Abduction

Draekon Destiny

Daughter of Draekons

Draekon Fever

Draekon Rogue

Draekon Holiday

Draekon Rebel Force with Lili Zander

Draekon Warrior

Draekon Conqueror

Draekon Pirate

Draekon Warlord

Draekon Guardian

Contemporary Romance

Royally Bad

Royally Fake Fiancé

Her Marine Daddy

Her Dueling Daddies

Beauty & The Lumberjacks

Snowed in with the Lumberjack

Rescuing Regina

Dark Mafia Romance

Mafia Brides

Revenge is Sweet

Vengeance is Mine

A Dark Mafia Romance trilogy with Stasia Black

Innocence

Awakening

Queen of the Underworld

Beauty and the Rose trilogy with Stasia Black

Beauty's Beast

Beauty & the Thorns

Beauty & the Rose

Cowboy Romance

Rocky Mountain Mail Order Brides

Rocky Mountain Dawn

Rocky Mountain Bride

Rocky Mountain Rose

Rocky Mountain Romp

Rocky Mountain Rogue

Rocky Mountain Daddy

Rocky Mountain Ride

Possessing Pearl

Wild Whip Ranch with Tristan River

Cowboy's Babygirl

Taming His Wild Girl

ABOUT THE AUTHOR

USA today bestselling author Lee Savino has written over 69 steamy romance novels. Bad boys, mafia men, wolf shifters, and dragon shifters in space—her dominant, alpha-hole heroes will stop at nothing to possess their one true love. Happily-ever-after and book hangover guaranteed!

Connect with Lee Savino in her fabulous Goddess Group: https://www.facebook.com/groups/LeeSavino